Skylar Mars

and the

Stolen Egg

by Drew Seren

See what Drew Seren is up to.

Visit his website www.drewseren.com

And sign up for his newsletter

Copyright 2018 © MysticHawker Press
http://www.mystichawker.com/

ISBN: 13: 978-1-945632-22-8

Edited by Cat Lauria
Cover design by Silver Circle Images

1
Raiders At Twilight

SKYLAR MARS stared at the upright display on his desk and ran his hand through his short brown hair. The answers to the test weren't coming as easily as they usually did. For the most part, he wasn't much more than an average student, but he didn't normally struggle on tests, even if Galactic History was one of his worst subjects. Frowning, he selected his answer. A large red X appeared on the screen. He was down two points on this question and only had two more choices. If he got the next one wrong, he'd lose all the points for the question and only be at fifty percent for the test so far. Around him, other students were quickly making their selections and progressing through the test.

Since one of the images displayed was a desert world, the remaining blue-green sphere had to be the aquatic world. A green check appeared on the screen with the word *Tursipia*, and he let out the breath he'd been holding. Galactic History was one of his worst subjects. He'd never been off-world and had little interest in venturing out beyond Hummassa. Sure, it was a bit backwater, but he liked knowing where everything was and most of the people in his small town of Cordnisar. He left the idea of exploring the cosmos to when he played video games.

As the next question popped onto the screen, Skylar glanced around the room. As in all his other classes that day, students were missing. Most of them were children of corporate workers who didn't really associate with him and the other world-bound kids, but it seemed odd. The corp-brats didn't miss class, not in unusually large numbers. The only kids remaining in school were either natives or kids like him, whose parents were too poor to ever think about leaving.

Shaking his head, he looked down at the next question. *Which of these beings most influenced the expansion of humans into the galaxy?* Four pictures stared at him. One was an old man with white hair that curled oddly at the ends. The next one looked more modern with a sleek, synthetic black suit and perfectly-styled black hair. Skylar knew he was the current human ambassador to the Central Galactic Council, but he couldn't remember the man's name. The third man had a rugged frontier look with a short brown beard, and long hair that looked like it would be awkward inside the old-fashioned space helmet under his arm. The fourth was a blue woman with overly-smooth skin whose large, dark eyes made her look like she came from a water world where the darkness of the depths made light scarce.

Skylar selected the rugged frontier guy. Another green check appeared with the name *Caffar O'Byrne*. Skylar nodded. He'd been the founder of O'Byrne Corporation. They had made intergalactic travel possible for humans nearly a thousand years earlier. Even though things had sped up considerably when they discovered stargate technology, and then other intelligent species, O'Byrne had been the one to get humans out of the Sol system, and the O'Byrne Corp was still a prominent player in the galaxy.

Feeling better about the test, Skylar got the next few questions easily. The final question appeared as the last bell sounded. Not really looking at his screen, Skylar touched a random answer and the green check mark appeared as his terminal shut down before his score displayed. He'd get his results the next day, but he wasn't worried. He stood and joined the flow of students heading out of school. The normal din in the hallway was even lower than it had been before the last class.

"Where is everyone?" asked Teir Puddle, Skylar's best friend and a native of the Hummassa, as they walked through the somewhat empty, utilitarian gray corridor.

"No clue," Skylar replied, feeling odd about not being jostled by the kids rushing to get out of school. "But if you stop and look, it's just the corp-brats. None of the Hummassan are missing and the rest of us regs are all here."

Teir nodded as they fell into step, heading away from school. The fresh air outside the school building was a welcome change from the overly-recycled air they were forced to endure for hours every day. "You're right. I wonder what's up. Maybe there's something special going on with their folks and they had to go along." A frown creased his dark red skin. "But I haven't heard about anything."

"Who knows?" It wasn't uncommon for the big corporations like O'Byrne to hold large events which all the employees and their families were required to attend. But from what Skylar knew, the missing kids' folks worked for several different corps. It was odd. A shiver ran through him. There was something there, but he couldn't think of what it meant. "So, what are you doing tonight? You want to meet me in-game later and we can see about killing a few slavers?" He and Teir spent most of their nights playing Galactic Explorers with people all over the galaxy. It gave Skylar little glimpses of what existence beyond Hummassa might be like. Teaming up with Teir was the best thing he'd done in-game, friends in real life and friends in-game. He couldn't image his life without Teir.

"Probably not." Teir hopped on one of the large boulders that had rolled down the hill overlooking the school after the last round of spring rains a month earlier. "I've got to get that hologram of the Orion cluster finished for art class. It's due tomorrow and I still don't have everything worked out. I really want this thing to pop."

"I can't wait to see it." Skylar smiled. He wasn't in Teir's art class. His mother didn't like the idea of his being too artsy. There wasn't much of a future in it. She kept him on a science path, which he didn't mind. His brain was better with figures and facts than fantasy, but he'd learned to appreciate some of the art Teir and his family produced. The native Hummassans were very creative, and some of their textiles and artwork were prized in other parts of the galaxy. "I'll try not to kill too many slavers without you. I've got to get home. Mom'll worry if I take too long. She's been watching me real close lately. It's almost like she's expecting me to grow another head or something."

Teir cocked a black eyebrow. "Do you have anything like that in your family tree?"

Skylar shrugged. "No clue." They reached the barely-defined path through the trees that led toward the modest adobe home he shared with his mother. "I'll see you tomorrow, then. Good luck with the hologram."

"Thanks." Teir chuckled. "Have fun with the slavers. I'll help you out with them tomorrow night."

AFTER DINNER, Skylar sat at his desk and touched the app on his terminal to link him to his homework. As the math questions popped up, his mind went back to Teir's question about his family tree. Over the past few years, he'd wondered about it himself.

Skylar didn't really know much about his father. His mom only said he was a great man who died in a horrible shuttle explosion sixteen years earlier, right before Skylar was born. She said he was human, but that was it. Maybe he had genes that might cause him to grow a second head.

Skylar didn't know much about his mother's side of the family either. She told him his grandparents were killed in a terraforming mishap while she was in college. The reason she'd moved to Hummassa was that it hadn't required terraforming, the natives were friendly, and they'd needed scientists and medical personnel to help their technology get up to the galactic standard. From the way the corp-brats complained about this world, it was still lagging behind, but Skylar didn't care. He liked Hummassa, even if he didn't have anything else to compare it to.

He glanced up at the large, holographic image on the wall above the head of his unmade bed. The scene he'd been told was an ancient mountain back on Sol Three, the last pure human home world, always relaxed him, despite a few glitches from the secondhand projector that sometimes let the rough wall show through the image. There was something calming in the way the colors played in the graphic. Moonlight illuminated the rough landscape, and he always thought there might be something hiding in the hologram's many shadows.

It was just an old picture—Sol Three had been abandoned nearly seven hundred years ago, right after the stargates were discovered and humanity left for the stars. There were lots of theories about what had happened, but the truth about Sol Three was shrouded in the past.

When he glanced back at his computer screen, there was an error message stating the link with the school computer had been lost. Skylar frowned at the screen and tapped the app to re-link with the school so he could complete his homework. Connections were often flaky, but normally came back up within a few seconds.

Connection not available at this time flashed across his screen.

He tried a couple more times before rebooting his tablet in hopes it would fix things. It didn't.

"Hey, Mom, is there a problem with the com-net?" Skylar shouted as he stood from the chair and headed for the hall.

"I don't know, Sky." His mom appeared in the doorway of their common room. She had already changed from her work clothes to her sleepwear. "What's happened?"

"I was trying to do my homework, lost my connection and can't get it back." He stopped where he was. Outside the short windows that ran the length of the hall, the long Hummassan twilight painted the sky with brilliant oranges and purples. In the distance, dots fell from the sky followed by frequent flashes of light. He pointed toward the horizon. "Mom, what's that?"

His mother hurried to his side. Her tanned face paled as she followed his gaze. "We're under attack. But who would attack Hummassa?"

The small house shook.

"They're hitting too close." His mother grabbed his hand. "We've got to get out of here. The office has shelters. We'll be safe there." Dragging him along, she ran for the front door.

A wave of external fear, unlike anything he'd ever felt before, hit Skylar before he could object. He was suddenly terrified to go outside. Somehow, it didn't feel like his own emotions. He was never afraid like that. Something bad was happening and he had no idea what to do. Shuddering, he didn't resist his mother pulling him along as they cleared the house. She was shaking violently and couldn't run in a straight line. He didn't need any other evidence to tell him she was terrified. She'd always been strong, but now, as someone dared to attack the quiet backwater planet they lived on, a fear stronger than anything he'd ever felt engulfed her and spilled over onto him.

They had a small hover car that was barely big enough for the two of them and a few bags of groceries. It hummed to life as they approached the small plastacrete pad outside the house.

A barrage of energy blasts hit the hillside behind their house. Not far away, smoke rose from the trees. Skylar remembered a house being in that direction, but had no way of knowing if it was the home burning or the jungle.

His mother released his hand. "Get in, quickly. We've got to get out of here."

"Mom, could this be why all the corp-brats left school today?" As he settled into his seat, the restraining harness clicked into place over his shoulders. He glanced at the house and wondered how much of it would still be there when they returned. His whole life was in that small house. They never had much; his mother always said it was bad to be overly attached to physical things. In that moment, he wondered if he was ever going to see any of his stuff again.

An unwanted vision of his home being the next one to burn entered his head. It was as sharp and clear as if he was standing on the hill near school looking down on it and the rest of Cordnisar. He'd heard about entire colonies being wiped out, but they were on the edge of the universe. There weren't any wars or anything going on. They should be safe… but they definitely weren't.

"The corp kids left school today?" A confused look crossed his mother's face as the hover car pulled onto the narrow dirt road leading away from the close-set houses of their neighborhood. "We did have an awful lot of people requesting off-world passage. Several of the ladies in processing complained about it over lunch."

Another round of blasts scorched the path in front of them, sending dirt and rocks flying in a large, dark wave.

"Hold on, Skylar." Her voice cracked as his mother jerked the control stick that manipulated the car's movement. Her fear spiked though him. They spun off the path and headed toward the thick trees. "Maybe I can lose them in the jungle."

"Lose who, Mom?" With shaking hands, Skylar clung to the door handle as the hover car careened through the landscape. He glanced about, expecting another round of fire at any moment. Trees could fall on them, or one of the barrages might hit the hover car and kill them both.

She didn't look at him like she normally did when she spoke. Her hand on the joystick turned white as she jerked it from side to side, moving through the trees. "These raiders. They aren't getting you."

Ahead of them, a tree exploded.

"What do you mean?" It didn't make any sense. "Why would they want me? I'm nobody." Confusion swirled around Skylar's fear. He wasn't anyone important. He was just a kid on a backwater world barely holding his own in school. Nobody was ever going to want anything with him.

He struggled to figure out what was happening. Leaves and limbs passed just inches from the car. Laser blasts lit up the night sky above him. Rocks and debris flew around and toward them. He couldn't think straight.

A tree crashed directly across their path. His mom pulled the stick back and the hover car shot over it. For a second, the darkening sky dancing with bolts of energy brightening the sky above the branches. The energy bolts were so bright they blocked out the stars, although the three small moons glowed dimly behind them. Then the car shifted back toward the ground.

His mother turned the car a different direction, heading deeper into the forest. "I swear, they aren't going to get you!" The frantic edge of her voice grew.

It sent shivers down Skylar's spine. He'd never heard her sound so scared. A vision that reminded Skylar of Galactic Explorers and the slavers he and Teir often fought in the game flashed through his head. Except instead of his game avatar, he saw himself and Teir being forced onto a ship and taken away.

With a huge lurch, the hover car swung madly as a bright light blinded him. Smoke filled the tiny compartment. Light from the car and the blasts around them illuminated the landscape, making them flash by in a weird cascade of light and shadow.

His mother let go of the joystick and grabbed his hand. "I love you, Skylar! Everything I've ever done, it was all for you!"

He squeezed her hand. Strange visions filled his mind. It made as little sense to him as everything else happening that night. He wished things would slow down enough he could sort things out. A tall, elegant man he'd never seen before appeared. Then there was a space station. Finally, their little house stood empty, waiting for them. "I love you too, Mom!"

The hover car hit something hard. The collision tore his mother's hand from his. An explosion shook them, and his seat launched through the windshield. "Mom!" He twisted in his seat, but the built-in safety features sent it flying away from the car. A force field engulfed him. He pounded against it as he and the seat tumbled through the broken night and shattered forest. Darkness engulfed him as his mother's voice filled his head. *"Skylar!"*

2
Blazing Jungle

THE HARSH smell of burning wood woke Skylar. Somewhere nearby, something exploded, and sparks showered down around him. One skidded across his blue synthetic shirt. The material was designed to resist burning, but reflexively, he brushed the ember away. For a moment, he glanced around the jungle, wondering where he was. He couldn't remember what happened.

He struggled, but the seat's harness still held him firmly. The memory of flying through the air as the hover car exploded came back. His mother had screamed his name.

Skylar hit the button to release the harness. The protective force field dissolved. The harness clicked, but didn't retract like it normally would. Yanking it off, he tossed it aside before he stood and looked about. The burning wreckage of the hover car still belched flames and smoke, and all around, the jungle burned.

Skylar ran back toward the hover car. A charred arm stuck out of the windshield.

"Mom!" he screamed. Everything seemed to close in on him until all he could see was her blackened limb, that hung unnaturally straight from the car like she was reaching out for him.

The fire roared up around him, pushing at him like a living thing. Skylar reached for his mom's charred hand, even though he knew she was dead. The smoke clouded the windshield, making it impossible for him to see through, and the only light he had was the fire that danced around the inside of the car.

Another explosion rocked the hover car. It blew Skylar backward, tossing him through the air. He landed roughly amid a rain of aluminum and Plexiglas parts. Pain shot through his spine and head. Struggling to his feet, he looked to where the hover car had been. Fire roared up the shattered trees around the small crater left behind. The power core had blown. There was nothing left.

As Skylar stared through tear-filled eyes at the place his mother had been, the fear that had enshrouded him during their flight through the jungle faded. He wanted to sit down and let the fire take him. His mother was the only family he had in the universe. He wasn't old enough to be a citizen on his own. Galactic law said he had to have a guardian until he was at least eighteen years old. He'd heard about what happened to orphans. There were more than a few tales, games and vids made about their exploits, and they were all tales of horror. It would have been better to die in the fire than end up in some home for wayward boys that was little more than a slave camp.

Overhead, one of the raider's ships fired another round. As he watched more trees blaze up, Skylar knew what he had to do. He was going to find out who they were. They had taken his mother, destroyed his life. Somehow, he was going to make them pay.

Willing his sorrow-filled tears back, Skylar squared his narrow shoulders and dashed off through the burning jungle. The thick black smoke curled around him, but he just plunged ahead, trying to reach the dim glow of the city. Someone there would know who the raiders were. If not there, he'd find out somehow. All the corp-brats had left, so their parents had to know something. One of the corporations must have discovered something useful on Hummassa and sent raiders to clear the place, so they could get access to it without having to negotiate with the natives.

Another energy blast cut through the jungle. Skylar spun as a huge tree crashed toward him. He tried to dodge, but a limb caught him across the side of the face and twisted him around. For the second time in minutes, he found himself on the ground as darkness descended.

BRIGHT LIGHT hurt Skylar's eyes as he slowly opened them. The jungle reeked of charred wood. He lay still for a moment. His head pounded, a sharp pain centering on his left ear. A throbbing ache radiated from his legs. A dull thudding across his skull made it hard to put thoughts together. With shaking fingers, he reached up and tried to find his ear. There was only about half of it left.

"No!" He had to get to the hospital. If he got there in time, they should be able to fix it. But his mother was gone; he didn't have anyone who could arrange his medical care. She was always the one who spoke to the doctors and nurses when he had to go in for anything. She'd made sure everything was okay. But she was gone. He'd seen her body before the power core exploded. There was no way she would be able to help him anymore.

He pushed at the tree pinning him to the ground, but it was heavy and lay right across his legs. Skylar wiggled his toes. They moved, and a sense of relief went through him. At least he wasn't going to be a paralyzed orphan.

"Hello, is there someone out here?" a woman's voice called in the distance.

"Over here!" Skylar shouted. Right after he did that, a bolt of fear hit him that the people who'd been shooting at the town might be the ones who found him. He was leading them right to him, but what choice did he have, pinned down and badly hurt? If the woman was with the attackers, then if she didn't shoot him, she would take him, and he'd know who they were, even if he did end up a slave.

"There, I've got you on sensor now." The woman sounded closer. "Don't worry. I'll get you out of here."

A wave of relief flooded Skylar as she came into view and he recognized the red shield on the woman's gray tunic. She was with Intergal Rescue, a group that traveled the universe helping those people who'd been through disasters both natural and sentient-made. He and his mother had volunteered with them during some unusually high flooding on the coast the previous summer. They were a source of light in the dark galaxy.

"Looks like you've got yourself into a bit of a fix there." The aid worker smiled. "Do you think your legs are broken?"

"I can wiggle my toes," Skylar replied. He was going to live, and that gave him a glimmer of hope. He'd wanted to die with his mother, but if he was going to live, then he could work toward finding the people responsible. It would become his life's work, no matter how long it took. They deserved to pay for what they had done to her and Cordnisar. The Hummassan were one of the most peaceful races in the universe.

"That's a good sign. Let's get you out from under there, and I'll scan you properly." She pulled off her silver backpack and took out a small jack, placing it under the tree trunk next to Skylar's leg. She removed a remote and hurried around to Skylar's head. "I'll yank you out." When she pressed a button, the jack lifted the downed tree two feet. She grabbed Skylar's shoulders and pulled him clear of the trunk.

"Thanks." Skylar started to get up but she put a restraining hand on his shoulder. His head swam, and he lay back on the ground.

"Stay there until I scan you." She straightened. "But let's get that tree back on the ground before it rolls and hurts one of us." She hit another button on the remote, and the tree lowered back down. Then the jack waddled out toward her.

Skylar watched the little robot move. "Why didn't you have it do all that on its own?"

"It's not that smart." She picked up the jack, returned the remote to its slot and put the tiny box into her backpack, exchanging it for a small hand-held scanner. "It's an older model. The newer ones can be commanded by voice, but these micro guys still require direct commands." She pointed the scanner at Skylar. "Do you live around here? Was anyone else with you?"

He nodded. "My mother and I live in the development at the southern edge of the jungle. She was with me, but our hover car blew up and she…didn't make it out." His lower lip quivered, and he fought to keep his voice steady. Tears ran out of his eyes. Somehow, talking about it made it so much more real. His gut clinched and he thought he was going to throw up. His mother was dead. He wasn't going to see her ever again. He was all alone in the universe. His throat closed up, and he struggled to get the words out. "There's a crater around here somewhere from when the power cell blew."

She frowned and the dappled sunlight glistened off the tear that rolled down her face. "I'm very sorry. Is your father on planet?"

Skylar shook his head. The motion made his ear hurt. "He died before I was born."

The aid worker looked at her scanner. "It doesn't look like your legs are broken, just bruised a bit. They'll probably be sore for a few days. Your ear on the other hand—let's hope we're in time to regenerate it. Did that happen last night?" She frowned at the scanner, as if not believing the reading. "It seems like it's already starting to heal."

"Yeah, when the tree fell on me." Skylar didn't mention that he tended to heal quickly. The family doctor had told his mother it must be something in his DNA, but they couldn't find anything definitive, and she'd refused to let them check too closely.

The woman glanced at the scanner again, then back at Skylar. "Have you had psi testing?"

He couldn't think of what to say. His mother despised psychics. Although most kids in the developed worlds were tested when they reached age eleven, his mother had used her position in the hospital records department to make sure he appeared on the negative report. He'd asked her about it at the time, when Teir had been tested too, and she had told him he didn't have to worry, that she'd taken care of it. If he said he'd somehow avoided the test, then it would raise questions. "I was negative," he lied. The odds were he'd never see the woman again; it wouldn't hurt to lie to her, even though he usually did his best to not lie to people.

The aid worker frowned and glanced at the scanner again. "That happens sometimes," she muttered before smiling at Skylar. "Okay, let's see if you can stand so we can get you out of here without calling for a pickup."

"So, what happens to me now?" Skylar stood. The world shifted slightly as the ache that had settled into his legs blossomed into full-blown pain again. He wobbled, and the aid worker caught his arm. A strange numb feeling washed over him. It was suddenly like nothing mattered but dealing with the pain in his body.

"Just stand there for a moment; let the legs get used to your weight." Eventually letting go of him, she slipped the scanner into her backpack and slung it over her shoulder. "We'll see if we can find you some family. There are very good odds that there's someone out there you're related to who'll take you in. You're almost old enough to be on your own."

As the pain dropped off to a sharp ache, Skylar shook his head. "I'm only fifteen."

"Then you're ready to go to school off-world. I bet that's what's going to happen to you." She glanced about. "Well, try a few steps. If it hurts too much, I'll call for a pickup. I need to keep scouring these woods. There may be more people trapped."

Skylar tried a few steps, and after the third one, the pain was at a level he could manage without wanting to cry out with each step. "I think I can make it."

"Good. The shuttles are going to be busy with folks a lot more banged up than you are." She began to walk back the way she'd come.

Skylar followed alongside her. For a moment, his gaze rested on the tree that had pinned him. It was the only tree in the visible forest that hadn't been burned. There was a slight mark on the end of the trunk where the raiders' laser had caught it, but beyond that, the leaves were still green and the bark still brown, unlike the trees around it that were deeply charred. He had gotten really lucky. "Do you know who did this?"

"We got the call from the Solar System Defense Network. The local enforcers said it was Boarisk raiders. Enforcement thinks they may have been after slaves. Over the past few years, the market for slaves has really taken off."

Skylar shuddered. He'd been talking to Teir about fighting slavers in a game, and then slavers came to Hummassa. In the game, the raiders would attack a city and haul off the people who were lucky enough to survive. He wondered how anyone could have survived the attack in better shape than he was. If he'd been unconscious when the slavers came through, was that why they'd left him behind? Had they thought he was dead?

The aid worker turned and looked at him. "You feel afraid. You don't need to feel afraid. I'll make sure everything you need is taken care of." Her words seemed to carry a sense of emotional disconnection, as if she were trying to make him numb to everything around him.

"Wait a minute." Skylar stared at the woman, trying to see what set her apart from normal humans. She looked to be from standard Sol stock, didn't even have any of the enhancements that so many families tried to splice into the genes of their offspring. "Are you a feeler?"

She nodded. "Only a low level. That's one of the reasons I work for Intergal Rescue. I can pick up just enough from strong emotions to find people who others might miss."

He'd never met a psychic before. Skylar frowned. "Doesn't it make you feel like a freak?" His mother had always made sure to keep them away from psychics. Most of the natives of Hummassa tested negative for psychic abilities. His mother had liked that about them. It wasn't natural for people to have psychic powers.

"Now you're afraid of *me*." Confusion etched the woman's brow. "What's wrong? I'm not going to hurt you. I'm trying to get you help."

"No." Skylar shook his head and took a couple of steps away from the woman. "Mom said we couldn't be around psychics. You're dangerous."

In that moment, he wasn't sure who was more dangerous—the feeler or the raiders. He wished his mother was there to help him figure out what to do, but this was his life now, and he had to make his own decisions.

The aid worker didn't *look* scary or dangerous. She looked like the other aid workers he and his mother had worked with to help find and save the flood victims.

She was just trying to do her job and save him.

The woman put her hands out in front of her. She wasn't reaching for Skylar. It looked more like she was trying to appear non-threatening. "It's okay. I'm not dangerous. I'm just a level two feeler. I'm not telepathic. You don't need to worry about me reading your mind. Most people who are afraid of psis are afraid of having their mind read. We need to get you to the aid center. Come on. Trust me, just for a little while, until we can get you to safety."

Looking around at the towering black pillars that had, the day before, been a thriving jungle, Skylar had to admit that she was right. He wasn't safe there in the remains of the woods. "Okay. But keep a good foot or more from me. I don't want you touching me again." He brushed at his shoulders where she'd pulled him free of the tree. It didn't feel like she'd done anything to him, but he couldn't be sure.

She sighed. "Let's get going. The sooner we get you to the aid center, the sooner I can get back out here and find people who *want* my help."

Skylar followed her. By the time they cleared the charred remains of the jungle, they were on the street that passed the school. The raiders' attack had done a real number on the buildings. Like the jungle and his mother's hover car, there wasn't much left. In the big playing field beside the devastated building, a series of bright white tents blew in the soft wind kicked up from a shuttle lifting off. People wearing gray jumpsuits emblazoned with the red shield hurried about.

The aid worker walked him over to the first tent. "Wait here. I'll let them know that you need to be taken to the hospital ship in orbit to see about repairing that ear.

I hope it's not been too long. There's already a fair amount of scar tissue."

Skylar ran his finger along the crusty, scabbed surface that marked the point where the rest of his ear was missing. It was one more thing the Boarisk raiders had taken from him.

3
Shot Off Into Space

SKYLAR SAT in the front of the tent for nearly an hour before anyone stopped for him. During that time, he watched a lot of people leave the tent in various states of injury. Most of them were hurried out to several shuttles that seemed to land right after the dust from the previous ship had settled. He quickly lost count of the number of people ferried to space. The enormity of the situation slowly sank in, and he wondered how many people were missing after the attack, and if it had been a world-wide assault or something focused on their small part of the large tropical planet.

At one point, he'd stopped one of the natives who wasn't in too bad a shape. "Excuse me, do you know if the Puddle family is okay?" Not knowing where Teir was gnawed at him. At least with his mother he knew what had happened to her. Teir was just an empty hole.

The frazzled old woman stared at him for a moment, then shook her head. "I don't know. So many lost."

"Do you have a com I could borrow to try and call them, to make sure they're alright?"

Sadness hit Skylar as the woman held up torn bleeding hands. "I'm sorry." She obviously had nothing beyond the freshly torn clothes on her back.

An Intergal worker stopped by and took the woman into the main tent. Skylar asked around for more information, but all he found out was that the local com network had been one of the first things taken out by the raiders and no one knew anything. Then it was his turn to go into the tent.

SKYLAR DID his best not to fidget as the Intergal nurse looked him over, but he wasn't used to anyone he didn't know poking at him like that.

The nurse let out a heavy breath. "I've seen worse, but you've already got a lot of scar tissue. I just hope it doesn't heal much more before we can get you to a regeneration station. I'd be tempted to put you in a cryotube but there aren't any available, and it's comparatively minor damage."

Skylar gripped the side of the cold metal examining table. "What happens if there's too much scar tissue?" He didn't want to go through life without part of his ear. He knew from biology class that the external ears of humans were just for focusing sound, so he'd still be able to hear, but he didn't want to be a freak. Everyone would know something horrible had happened to him. Even if they gave him a fake ear, someone would be able to tell it wasn't real. He just knew it.

She waved dismissively. "We'll just have to shave the scar tissue off. If there's too much new growth, it'll impact the way the ear grows back. If we trim the ear, the new tissue'll grow back in closer to the way it was."

Skylar leaned back and glared. The jumble of emotions he'd been feeling since he'd been rescued bubbled to the surface. "Really? If it's not growing right, you cut it off, try again and hope it looks better? I'm not a plant, you know. You can't just trim off what you don't like." Anger surged out of him and he wanted to get off the table and storm out of the tent. Maybe he could go live in a swamp with a deformed ear and plot his revenge on the Boarisk until he was old and gray.

"Mr. Mars, it would really help if you could just remain calm." Her brown eyes suddenly widened and the tired look left her face. She looked like she was about to run, like something had scared her. "Everything *will* be fine."

"Really?" Skylar had been trying to keep his cool. Ever since being brought to the camp by his empathic rescuer, his stress and sorrow at losing his mother and not being able to find out anything about Teir had been slowly replaced by anger. Now, in the guise of the nurse with a less than acceptable bedside manner, he'd found an outlet. "Are you going to take what's left of my mother and pop her into a regeneration chamber and grow me another mom? Are you going to find all the people who're missing after last night's raid? I don't think so!" He hopped off the table and started toward the cloth door that led out of the tent. "I'm so out of here!"

The woman who'd found him in the forest appeared in his path. Behind her stood a burly man with a brown furred face and the bright, slitted, yellow eyes of a Pantherian. "Skylar, I understand your agitation, but we're about ready to get you to the orbital hospital ship. If you can just calm down."

He stared at his rescuer. He was getting tired of people telling him to calm down. "Who says I want to leave this planet? Maybe this is my home! Can you make me leave here?"

She winced like he'd just hit her.

The burly cat-man stepped around her. "Son, you need to calm down. Your anger isn't helping anyone here." His gaze bore into Skylar's.

Something in that look stabbed through him. His agitated mind dulled. Skylar gulped as his anger drained away, leaving only a hollow spot where fires had burned moments before. "What are you?"

The smile that crossed the man's furry face appeared almost predatory, but there was a soft friendliness to it. "A level ten feeler. The strongest empath we have on planet right now. I think you need to relax and let us get you up to the med ship. Hopefully, we'll find a relative to connect you with."

Deep inside, Skylar wanted to keep his anger. The anger gave him something to hold on to so he didn't break down, but with the emotional control radiating from the Pantherian, he could only nod. He realized why his mother had been so wary of psychics: they could literally make you do things you didn't want to do. They were dangerous.

The cat-man looked at the nurse. "Is he ready for the next shuttle?"

The nurse nodded. "There's nothing more I can do for him here. There are others that need my attention."

The Pantherian gestured for the nurse to leave. "Then we'll take it from here."

Once the nurse left, the big cat man squatted down on the floor in front of Skylar. Being on the same level made Skylar feel more like they were equals. "Skylar, you've got a lot of anger in you. I understand it. The horrors the Boarisk perpetrate are just unthinkable. But there'll be time for your vengeance later. That is what you want, isn't it, vengeance?"

Skylar nodded as he leaned back against the examining table. "Yes, sir." He couldn't believe he was being forced to be calm, almost sedated. It didn't feel right. He felt like he was betraying his mother with his reaction, but there was nothing he could do about it.

"Good, that's a healthy response. Don't ever forget it, but don't let it eat you alive either. You'll learn control. When the time comes, I have no doubt you'll make those raiders pay for what they've done here." The Pantherian extended digits that were more like a paw than a human hand. "Now, we didn't get formally introduced. I'm Philaneo Clawson, most people just call me Phil."

Skylar's anger receded further back as he took Phil's hand. Even his fear of psychics faded. It was the first time he'd ever touched a Pantherian. The fur under his fingers was soft and silky. "Thanks, Phil. I'm Skylar, but I guess you already knew that."

Phil inclined his head. "That I did. But it's nice to make it formal. Gina told me about your loss. I'm sorry." Phil straightened up. "I need to ask Gina a couple of questions before she goes back out to look for more survivors. She's got the coordinates of your home, and she'll handle the salvage once rescue phase is complete. I'll be going up to the hospital ship with you, so I'll be right back."

Numbly, Skylar nodded. "Okay. So, we're leaving soon then?" He wanted to get fixed up, but beyond that, he wasn't sure what he wanted to do. Everything was muddled. At least someone would be checking his home for anything that had survived the attack.

"On the next shuttle. I'll be right outside if you need anything." He gestured to Gina and the two of them walked out, leaving Skylar feeling more tired than anything else.

He eased back up on the examining table, since there wasn't anywhere else to sit. With a deep breath, Skylar tried to relax. As quiet descended and the pounding of blood in his ears dropped, he found he could hear Phil and Gina on the other side of the tent flap. Even though he could tell they were trying to keep their voices down, they were close to the thin fabric and their conversation carried to him.

"You were right to get me in here, Gina," Phil said. "The boy is really strong for his age."

"He was more than I could handle. I'm just sorry the nurse set him off before I could get here. Any idea what we're going to do with him?" Worry colored her voice. "We can't turn him loose on an unsuspecting galaxy."

"Have you gotten anything back from the DNA inquiry?"

"Just a mitochondrial match to the woman whose remains were found in the jungle. I'd say his mother. It matches his story. Haven't had time to check official documents for things like wills and such. Too much going on."

Skylar gulped. Inside, he knew he should be crying at the confirmation of his mother's death, but the strange emotional slump Phil had put him in wouldn't allow even that. He was too numb. What did they mean by "really strong?" He wasn't any stronger than any other human boy his age. There was too much coming at him too quickly. It was getting very confusing.

"There's time for that later. What about a match for his sire? Surely the boy has a father."

"I've been trying, but there's some kind of black hole in that data. Actually, for the mother too. It's like someone has purposely removed them from the galactic database. That or they were both born on a primitive world, but he's obviously human. From the look of him, I'd say he can trace his ancestry back to Sol Three without even trying. He doesn't have any of the trace sequences we normally find in any of the known engineered species."

Phil sighed. "Well, we've got to find somewhere safe for him. Luckily, Intergal has authority to place orphans when we need to. When they go through the local computers, let me know if his mother made any arrangements for him. Until then, I'll handle things. Once I get him up to the hospital ship and they do a regeneration session, I'll make some calls. I think I know somewhere that might be perfect for him."

"That would be good. He needs someone on his side."

"I have a soft spot for pure humans, you know that."

Gina giggled. "I know. I better get back out there. So far, we've only got about twenty-five percent of the area searched. Still haven't gotten to the swamps west and south of town. The jungles to the north are thick and people may have fled there. We might find a few survivors."

A tiny spark of hope lit in Skylar's chest. Teir's family was in the northwest side of the city. Not far from where he lived, where the jungle and swamp came together. There might be a chance they were still alive.

"The Boarisk raiders probably took off with the rest of them," Phil continued. "There's been chatter all over the communications channels that they're hitting planets in this area looking for the able-bodied. Something about needing more workers on some new mining planet."

"Slavers." The word sounded like she forced it out from between clenched teeth.

Their voices dropped below what Skylar could hear. A shiver went through him. Everyone knew that slavery was wrong, but that didn't stop raiders from taking slaves, particularly from backwater worlds like Hummassa. But Skylar was more interested in what the Intergal Rescue folks were going to do with him. Was she right and he was 'pure' human? His mother had never even hinted that might be the case. Even most of the corp-brats had some kind of gene-manipulation done to them that made them less…or more…than human.

Before Skylar could ponder very long, Phil came back in. "You about ready to go? The shuttle's back and loading."

"I guess." Skylar slid off the table. He surveyed the white canvas walls and grass floor. It felt like he should have something to take with him, but everything he owned was back at home, the house he and his mother fled the previous night. All he had left was himself. He didn't even have a home anymore.

SKYLAR LOOKED around as he followed Phil out of the room. He'd been in regeneration therapy for nearly half a day. When his ear had failed to grow back perfectly, the doctors suggested cutting it back and trying again. It was the first thing since he'd met Phil that he'd been able to work up the emotional energy for, and he rejected the idea.

It surprised him that Phil backed him, even after Phil explained that he could feel how important it was to Skylar to keep the scarred ear. As they walked down the sleek, sterile hallway, Skylar kept glancing at the new top of his ear in every reflective surface they passed. It was withered and slightly pointed. It was his first scar.

"If you let your hair grow a bit, it'll help hide it," Phil suggested.

Skylar shook his head. "I don't want to hide it. I want it out there for the world to see. I want to see it every time I look in the mirror so I don't ever forget what happened on Hummassa." Not that he thought he could forget, unless some telepath went in and wiped the memory from him, and he wasn't about to let that happen.

"Don't worry, I don't think you'll forget." Phil turned down a wider hallway. Skylar obediently followed. "You've got one of the strongest wills I've ever encountered in a human. I don't have any doubts that you're going to be a force to be reckoned with in the galaxy. Just don't let your need for vengeance get the upper hand over your intelligence."

"I'll try." Skylar didn't know where they were going. Phil had been vague when he'd come out of the chamber, but the Pantherian seemed happier than he was when Skylar went into the regeneration session.

"So Skylar, you said on the ride up here you'd never been off-world before. I guess it's safe to say that you've never been through a stargate either."

Skylar nodded. "Yes, sir." In school, he'd learned about the stargates that connected most parts of the galaxy. His mother often said she wished she could share the experience with him, but claimed they couldn't afford a trip that entailed the use of a gate. It had sounded like a lot of fun when some of the corp-brats at school talked about the trips their parents would take them on to distant spots in the galaxy. The graphics of going through a stargate were awesome in Galactic Explorers.

"Then you're in for a treat." Phil stopped at a doorway.

At the end of a short hall stood a heavy-duty door. It sealed that section of the medical ship from the airlock behind it. Past the airlock, Skylar hoped there was a ship. There weren't any windows in the door, so he couldn't see what lay beyond it, but it looked like the one they'd come through when they took the shuttle up from the surface.

"Where are we going?" Skylar asked as Phil entered a code into the numeric pad by the door.

"I'll let that be a surprise for now." Phil smiled. A wave of calm, like the ones that had hit him back on the planet, washed over him. It didn't dull the excitement that was building in him about the trip through the stargate, but it did push aside the building questions about where they were headed. "But I think you're going to like it. It'll be interesting, at least until we can find some family for you to make the decisions that really need to be made right now."

The door rolled open with a slight *whoosh*, revealing the short airlock behind it. Once they were through, Phil closed the first door before opening the second. "We'll use my personal ship for our little trip."

That took Skylar by surprise. He'd never known anyone who had his own ship before. "Your ship? That's really cool."

"Not really. It's a perk of being a level ten feeler." After they both cleared the second door, Phil closed the outer airlock, which was bright and hospital clean, and the ship door which had a nasty scorch mark across it. "I never know when I'll be needed somewhere. There aren't a lot of level tens in the galaxy in any of the psi talents. There are only a hundred or so feelers, a few dozen readers and less than ten movers that are level tens. Those of us who decide to use our gifts for the good of the many and work for Intergal or other, neutral, aid organizations get yanked around a lot. To make it easier, we get our own ships. The ones who just want to use their gifts to line their own pockets…well, they have ships too, they're just fancier than ours." He chuckled as the lights came on. "It would be nice if the ship came with a crew, but luckily flying this little beauty isn't as hard as a big ship. The nav computer does most of the work for me."

Skylar couldn't think of what to say. The ship wasn't as shiny and clean as the hospital ship, but had a nice, lived-in atmosphere to it. It was comfortable—like Phil made him feel. His concern about Phil being a level ten feeler didn't seem as important as what was about to happen. He was about to go into space. His life was changing fast, and he suddenly wanted to be ready for all of it.

The first room was obviously the galley and seating area. There was a small food dispenser with a few colorful drips running off its silver front edge. Several chairs were stacked high with clothing. For a moment, Skylar was acutely aware of his lack of belongings. His blue synth shirt and pants were battered, but at that point, along with his synthleather shoes, they were the extent of his possessions. He didn't have any money, so he wasn't sure how he was going to get anything else.

Phil cut in before he could dwell on it. "So, do you want to join me on the flight deck, or would you rather ride back here? Some people don't like watching the stars go by."

Right at that moment, there was nothing Skylar wanted to do more than star gaze. "If there's room for me in the pilot's cabin, that would be great." He'd been in simulators, but he suspected they were nothing like really going into space.

"Okay, but it might get a little boring. We're a few hours from the nearest gate. The one for Hummassa is a couple of planets over for some reason, not in lunar orbit to the populated planet like a good number of them. Overall this is going to be about a twelve-hour trip." Phil strolled toward the door Skylar assumed led to the flight deck. "But don't worry. I'm fully stocked with food. My dispenser will do any cuisine you can think of, even though I don't get passengers very often."

The deck had three plush flight chairs, two of which sat near the window that looked out onto the stars before them. The hospital ship filled the left portion of the window, but beyond that, a tapestry of stars spread out before them. The instrument panels stood in front of both chairs. They appeared to be standard touchscreens. Here and there, dark scuff marks marred the off-white edges, evidence Phil tended to rest his hands and arms on the rims when using the controls. At the moment, the panels were unlit, obviously waiting for Phil's commands.

Phil sat in the left chair, and Skylar hopped into the right. The excitement for his first stargate trip bubbled up in him. It was really going to happen! He wished his mom were here with him.

His throat and chest tightened, but then a numb feeling swept over him. It was almost like he *couldn't* grieve. It didn't feel right, but the excitement of leaving the planet he'd always called home pushed it away.

As the control panels lit up, Phil touched some buttons. "Hospital Ship Curry control, this is Philaneo in Rescue Paw One. I'm ready for departure from docking port thirty-four."

Skylar couldn't hear anything, but he didn't expect to. When Phil tapped his fingers together, he realized the Pantherian must have a sub-dermal communications device. A lot of the corp-brats had them, but most of the populace of Hummassa still relied on older forms of communication, either video- or radio-based.

"Thanks," Phil said. "I guess I'll see you guys in a couple of days unless they need me elsewhere." The ship shook slightly. Skylar leaned forward in his seat, hoping to see the airlock retracting from the ship, but it was too far back. He suddenly wished the med shuttle he'd flown up to the bigger ship in had been designed to have windows. He'd missed everything on the way up.

He straightened in his seat and stared wide-eyed as they drifted away from the hospital ship. The stars didn't look any closer, but there was a strange feeling of distance between them and the larger vessel. For a moment, Skylar wondered if space would just be able to swallow them whole.

Taking the yoke that slid out from under the panel below the control screens, Phil chuckled. "That's nothing. Sit back and enjoy the ride." Then the little ship shook again and started moving away from the hospital ship. When the bulk of the other ship was behind them, the view of the stars really opened up. They were moving slowly enough for Skylar to make out some of the constellations he was familiar with. They all looked much brighter and more colorful without Hummassa's atmosphere distorting them. He glanced around wanting to see everything possible. There was so much to see he wasn't sure he could ever see everything.

"We're lucky this is a small system," Phil said as he touched a series of places on his control panel. "In some of the larger, underpopulated systems, it can take a day or more to go from the inner planets to the stargate when they aren't in lunar orbit. It also helps that the stargate and Hummassa are on the same side of the sun right now. The calculations would be a bit trickier if we had to navigate around the sun."

"Is it hard to learn to fly one of these?" Skylar asked. In that moment, as they flew away from the planet he'd called home for all of his fifteen years, he knew he wanted to learn to fly spacecraft. Even with the weight of his mother's loss still present, he felt free.

He'd heard some of the other kids talk about wanting to go into space when they were old enough, signing onto any passing ship needing extra hands, but he never really understood until he experienced space for himself. There was something incredible about being off the planet, with the universe opening up before him. He wondered how hard it would be for him to get a ship and just make space his home. Maybe he'd never have a house and family, but he could have a ship and possibly a crew. It would make hunting Boarisk easier.

"With the modern nav-coms, it's fairly easy." Phil settled back in his chair and let go of the control yoke. "Centuries ago, when the Central Galactic Council was still forming and setting up the stargates and their tech, it was a different thing. Back then, the pilot had to do all the calculations to make sure you didn't accidently fly through a sun, black hole, or asteroid belt. There're still a few places where you have to use manual. Not all of the galaxy is completely charted." A faraway look crossed Phil's furry face. "There're still places that need exploring. I wish I had more time for that." He turned and looked at Skylar. "Kid, if you get the chance, explore the universe. There's nothing like going somewhere no known species has ever been."

"That sounds cool," Skylar said. "I feel like I belong out here." The darkness wasn't scary. It felt welcoming, like he was finally home.

"A lot of us feel that way. There's a lot that's easier in space. You'll find that out over the next few years."

"What do you mean? Aren't you taking me to another planet?" Then he realized Phil hadn't said much about where they were going. Said it was going to be a surprise. If it was going to be as cool as the ship flying through space was, he was ready for it. Anything that helped him not dwell on his past life was going to be a good thing.

Phil shook his head. "Nope. I'm taking you to a space station. Right now, that's all I'm going to tell you. I've made arrangements for you to stay there until your kin are found. If you're lucky, even after we know who they are, they'll let you stay. I think you'll learn a lot there. I know I did."

"Learn a lot? Like what kind of stuff?" It sounded to Skylar like Phil was taking him to some kind of school, but he'd never heard of a school in a space station. Then he realized that the way his mother protected him from so much, there was probably a lot he'd never heard of out there.

"All kinds of stuff. Just wait and see." Phil pointed at something outside the window. "There's Barrose, the largest gas giant in this system. You'll get a better look at it over the next hour until we clear its gravity well. We're trying to arc around it, but if we go too far, we add a couple of hours to our flight anyway."

The huge green and purple planet was little more than a ball, but it grew larger with each passing minute. Skylar watched it grow. It was so different from the vids he'd seen, or the games he played where he flew past a planet. It was more real, more interesting. From school, he knew there were four moons orbiting the planet. He searched for them and spotted two.

Barrose was the only planet they passed closely. That didn't deter Phil from pointing out the various astronomical things they could see. There were three comets, one of which seemed to be traveling the same path they were, but it quickly fell behind once they cleared the gas giant's gravity well and hurled toward the stargate. Skylar's breath caught when they finally came within sight of it. For a moment, it looked big enough for Hummassa to fit inside it.

It was a perfect circle with made of huge silver blocks that looked almost square, until he peered as hard as he could at one and realized the lower edge was ever-so-slightly curved and fit together flawlessly. Skylar had never heard of any ship being too big to fit through a stargate, and considering he figured small planets could fit through the one he was staring at, it made sense. The thing was massive.

"We'll be there in about half an hour," Phil announced. "If you want anything to eat, or if you need to pee before we go through, now's the time."

Skylar shook his head. "Nope, staying right here." Even though he'd been sitting in the seat for eight hours, and had only pried himself away for one really fast trip to the bathroom, there was no way he was leaving his chair. They were about to go through the stargate and he was going to see every little detail of it.

"All right. Tell you what, let me check back in with Intergal and see if there's any news of your friend." Phil tapped a couple of times on one of the panels that had gone dark after they left the hospital ship.

Skylar wasn't sure if he should hope for new or not. He didn't want to know Teir was dead, missing was better than dead. It at least gave him something to hope for.

"Hey, Reg, this is Phil, wanted to see if you have an updated survivor or"—he paused and sighed—"or casualty list."

It was hard to wait for a response he couldn't hear. Skylar wanted to be able to listen in, but that would be rude. If Phil hadn't put the call on the ship coms, there was a reason.

"Good, if you could check for a Teir Puddle for me. He's a native, not a worker." Phil paused again. He pointed out the view port. "Not long now. Sorry this is taking so long."

"Thanks for checking." Skylar's throat was tight with fear of what Phil might find.

"Gives us something to do while we approach the stargate." Phil touched his lips. "Thanks Reg. I'll keep checking in from time to time, or if you could put a note in the system to contact me if we get a definitive. Will do. Thanks again." He tapped the panel again and it returned to its dark, inactive state. "Sorry, Skylar, no news yet."

"Then there's still hope." Skylar stared at the stargate getting close and closer. He tried to recall the number of times he and Teir had gone through one in game. It was too many to count. He wondered how Teir would feel about going through one for real.

4
Through The Stargate

THE HUGE ring floated in space. It was held in place by a series of complex gravimetric systems that always made sure the gate stayed in a relative position to a nearby moon or star. If a gate was out of position, even by a small amount, it could dramatically affect ships coming and going through it, possibly in catastrophic ways.

As Phil's fingers danced across the control panel in front of him. Tiny bolts of lightning flared out from the ring blocks, cascading toward the middle of the ring. The sparkling continued until it filled the dark space in the ring's center, effectively blocking out the stars beyond it.

"I would say 'hold on,' but the jump beyond the event horizon isn't extreme in terms of bumpiness," Phil said. He took his hands off the steering yoke and for a moment, the ship drifted before the artificial gravity field of the gate caught hold of it. "You know, we're lucky Intergal agents get free passage through the gate system. When you take cruises and other commercial flights, they have a charge built into their ticket costs to cover the gate energy fee.

"I guess the Galactic Council thought of everything when they built the gates," Skylar said. His mother never had kind things to say about the Central Galactic Council that ran the Milky Way Galaxy.

"Yeah. Although there are a lot of people who think the gates paid for themselves decades ago and are just a way for the corporations to line their pockets now." Phil didn't turn his attention from the stargate.

Skylar held his breath as everything blurred around them. When they passed the edge of the gate, the little ship sped up beyond anything it had done in normal space. His heart thudded against his throat and his palms got so wet that he had to wipe them on his pants.

The stargate pulled them into a constructed wormhole that carried them nearly instantly from one side of the galaxy to the other. Then a shimmer of energy appeared in front of them as they exited the wormhole, and darkness dotted with stars returned to the view outside the window.

Taking hold of the yoke again, Phil sighed. "Well, that was the exciting part. Kinda anticlimactic after you've done it a few times."

With his heart still pounding, Skylar shook his head. "I can't see where that would ever get boring. That was so cool! I can't wait to do it again."

"I'm sure you will." Phil chuckled. "It's rare nowadays for people to stay isolated on worlds like Hummassa. Some of us land on a different world every week or so. Why don't you run back and grab us something to drink? We've got an hour or so before we reach our destination."

"Okay." Skylar got out of his seat and headed to the cabin door. Although if the flight into wherever Phil was taking him was like the flight from the med ship to the gate, there would be little things like comets, asteroids, planets and other common space phenomena to pass near, but nothing like the gate. Nevertheless, Skylar wanted to hurry and get back in his seat. Space was a lot more exciting than he'd expected it to be. From what he'd heard, most of the larger ships tourists used weren't designed for sightseeing, but for getting people from one point to another. "Just don't do anything interesting without me here."

"I'll try not to."

TRY AS he might, Skylar couldn't stay awake and after nearly ten hours of flying through space, he dozed off. In his dreams, he still saw his mother's arm sticking out the windshield of the hover car right before it exploded. A tall, dark-haired man who looked a bit like Skylar laughed as he walked through the flaming wreckage. Somewhere nearby something inhuman screamed. The man held out his hand as Skylar jerked awake.

"Hey there." Phil frowned from the pilot's chair. "Not that it helps much, but nightmares might be part of your sleep for a while. You've been through a lot lately. I'm sure we can find a way to dull them if you like."

Yawning, Skylar shook his head. He didn't want anyone to help him out by messing with his head. He'd endure the nightmares if he had to.

"Okay. If you change your mind, any of the teachers will be able to point you in the right direction." Phil waved out the main port. "We're almost there. You can just make out the academy."

Skylar sat up straighter and peered into the velvety space beyond the window. Another gas giant dominated his view of the stars. "Where is it?"

Phil pointed to the upper right side of the window. "It's over there. Look for the multi-colored flash. See it, just past the gas giant?"

Skylar stared in the direction Phil indicated. There beyond the indicated planet, seeming to be in orbit with a smaller green and blue planet, and looking more like a small flattened moon with a hole in the middle than a space station, was a spinning disk. It wasn't like any of the pictures Skylar had seen of space stations in textbooks. As it moved, sunlight from the single yellow star glistened off something that looked like it should be part of the station.

"What's that?" Skylar pointed as another ray of light flashed in the distance.

Phil looked. "Oh, I bet you're seeing the light reflecting off the solar collectors. The academy is mostly self-sufficient. That helps it stay neutral."

Skylar looked from the station to Phil. "Neutral? Aren't we still in Council space?" He knew it was a silly question. The Central Galactic Council controlled all of the human-settled parts of the Milky Way Galaxy and was actively spreading their influence to other galaxies as they established more stargates.

"We are. But there are people from many different planets at the academy. They strive to provide the best education, regardless of race, species, planet, or social standing. Other establishments over the years have tried to do what they do here, and problems always arose because one sect or another would attempt to gain an upper hand. It never ends well, even when the Council steps in. Things have gone along fairly smoothly for the past three hundred years, so as long as the academy can maintain a level of neutrality—"

Skylar interrupted, slumping in his seat. "The place is three hundred years old?" In the back of his mind, he'd hoped that by getting off Hummassa, he'd get to experience some newer technology. Finding out their destination was a three-hundred-year-old space station let some of the excitement out of that expectation.

"Yeah, but don't worry, they're really good at what they do."

"And what is that exactly?"

"Giving young minds an opportunity to grow and become the strongest and best people they can."

Skylar frowned. "That's a bit vague." The feeling of Phil manipulating his emotions had fallen to the back of his mind, but it was still there. With his less-than-complete answers, Skylar wondered what all he was hiding. Unfortunately, he really wasn't in any position to complain about things. Phil was showing him some of what the universe could offer him and he didn't want to do anything to upset that.

Phil shrugged. "You'll find out more once we dock and you get to meet the staff." He turned the yoke and the ship banked. "Tell you what—why don't I give you a flyby before we dock?" He tapped his thumb and forefinger. "This is Philaneo Clawson requesting a flyby before docking. I believe we're expected." There was a slight pause. "Yes, it is just me and Skylar Mars, the youngster we sent you the info about, on board." During the next pause, the academy grew large enough to easily make out the clear inner ring covering a green space. "Thank you. We'll be at Airlock Three in five minutes."

He banked the ship around again, swinging lower until they were only a few hundred yards from the station's surface. "Here we go."

The first thing Phil did was fly through a gap where a clear sphere hung in the center of the station, connected by metal girders to a transparent tube. To his right, several people floated about the sphere. To his left, a vast green space included what looked to be playing fields. Trees filled one part of the green with a stream meandering through a forest as well as large greenbelt. The stream ended in a large lake or swimming pool of some sort. Near several large buildings, cows wandered in a fenced-off area.

"Wow, this is awesome," Skylar said, without pulling his eyes away from the spectacle before him. He didn't want to miss even the smallest detail.

"Stars' End is a great place." Phil turned the yoke slightly to avoid a small bot that floated between the two dark areas. "These areas are currently just in the shadow of an asteroid."

They passed back into open space. The sun was right in front of them. Phil swung the ship around and skimmed low over the sunward surface. A vast field of solar panels sparkled in different colors. It was older technology, but still efficient. A fair number of the cities on Hummassa used solar technology.

Their view of the station darkened when they reached its edge, and Phil piloted the ship away from the sun. The dark side of the station was covered with a myriad of windows. From the glimpses Skylar caught, some looked into classrooms, some into private areas, and many weren't lit at all, just dark panes along the surface. Other lights of various colors were along the station's outer skin, most small and stationary, but a few moved around. Skylar didn't understand what they all meant, but the overall display left him speechless. Stars' End wasn't like any space station he'd ever seen pictures or video of. He wondered if it was one of a kind.

As they swung back around, a series of yellow lights blazed before them. They seemed to extend into space on long delicate poles where they formed a circle on the surface of the station.

"There's our airlock," Phil announced. A light flashed on his control panel and he took his hands off the yoke. "Best to let the station complete the docking for us."

More lights came on across the station near their port, illuminating several other docked ships. Most appeared to be about the same size as Phil's ship. There were two larger ships that looked like they could hold a lot of people.

Shortly after the ship stopped moving, there was a soft click from back in the ship, near the airlock. Phil smiled and patted the arms of his chair. "So, are you ready for your next adventure?"

Skylar nodded. "Sure, let's do it." He couldn't wait to see what was going to happen next.

5
Stars' End Academy

PHIL OPENED the second airlock door and gestured for Skylar to step through into the room beyond. "Skylar Mars, welcome to Stars' End Academy, the finest school in the galaxy for budding psi talents."

His words brought Skylar up short. He'd just been brought to one of the most dangerous places in the universe, if his mother was to be believed. So far Phil hadn't done anything more than calm him, as had Gina back on Hummassa. He didn't think either one of them had any nefarious designs on him, but he wasn't sure. While he was there, he'd stay on his guard as well as he could, but he didn't have any real choice of where else to go unless Phil or someone else was able to find his family. If he didn't know Intergal was a force of good in the galaxy, he'd have been far more worried, but he believed they would do their best to make sure he was properly taken care of until a better opportunity came along. Without a family, he was under their control until he was old enough to legally be on his own.

Squaring his shoulders, Skylar followed Phil. The room was larger than Skylar had expected. It was nearly twice the size of the school cafeteria back on Hummassa. Other than a few doors and openings into hallways, it was a large, empty space that reminded Skylar of a stadium without seats. There were a number of holograms on the walls of various people, most in formal dress, not all of them human. Every race Skylar had ever heard about, and a few he hadn't, were depicted there.

The room's lush carpet felt like grass under his feet as he stepped further inside. Everything had an expensive but used feeling to it. If the school was as old as Phil had said, that made sense.

What surprised Skylar most was the lack of people. The only person in the room was a tall, older woman who was currently walking toward them. She was dressed casually, in a long skirt and colorful blouse, looking more like someone who should be on a rural planet as opposed to a space station where he expected jumpsuits or business suits like he always saw on the NPCs on space stations in Galactic Explorer. Something about the way she moved reminded him of one of his mother's bosses, who was always a bit distant even when she was trying to be nice.

"Phil, you didn't give me time to get here," she fussed as she tapped something on the tablet in her hands. "I thought you were going to do a flyby."

Phil flashed her a warm smile, far warmer than anything he'd shown Skylar. "I did take the time to show Skylar the outside of the station. Maybe next time I'll make a couple of orbits to give you the opportunity to get to the entrance hall and receive your newest charge."

"Maybe you should." She smiled back before turning her attention to Skylar. "So, you're Skylar Mars. Phil and Gina contacted me about you. You've been through a lot the past couple of days. Hopefully, we can help you out here at Stars' End while we're working on finding your family." She offered her hand to Skylar.

With a little trepidation, he grasped her fingers lightly.

"Welcome, Skylar." Her voice rang in his head. *"I'm Fiona Grissom, the head counselor. I think you're going to fit in here just fine."* She looked at Phil. "You were right to bring him here. We'll take good care of him. Are you going to be able to stay around for a bit? I

think we have a few students who might enjoy talking to a level ten feeler."

Skylar wanted to let go of her hand and run back to Phil's ship, but he pushed the feelings down and continued her handshake, hoping his face didn't betray the shock he felt at her voice in his mind.

Phil shook his head. "Sorry, but those raiders did a real number back on Hummassa. They need me there. I would've waited until the immediate problems were over, but Gina and I both felt Skylar should be in your care as soon as possible."

Fiona frowned. "It's a shame you can't stay. But thank you for getting Skylar to us." She glanced about. "Skylar, don't you have any bags or anything of your own?"

"No, Ma'am." No matter how uncomfortable talking to her was, he wasn't going to be impolite. That was a bigger disservice to his mother's memory than being in Fiona's presence was. "I presume our house was destroyed in the raiders' attack."

"We have the coordinates of his home," Phil said. "Once the recovery is complete, we'll find what we can salvage. I'll see that it's sent to him here, or if any family has been found by then, we'll send it there."

"Then we'll have to see what we can find for you here at the academy." Fiona tisked. "There's always a few extra of everything around here. Maybe I can see about getting you planet-side one of these days to see if we can find you a few personal items. I think every species understands the need to have a few things that are just yours."

"Then I should be off." Phil started to turn back to his ship. "Fiona, if you would be so kind to convey my greetings to my niece and let her know I'm sorry I couldn't stay long enough to say hello. Also, ask her to keep an eye on our boy here. Skylar, hang in there. The folks here are awesome and I know Fiona will go out of her way to make you feel at home."

"Thanks, Phil." He couldn't think of anything else to say. He'd been picked up and flown across the galaxy to a totally strange space station full of psychics he was terrified to be left with and the only person he'd felt comfortable with was leaving, probably for good. He'd never felt more alone in his life.

With a parting wave, Phil hurried into the airlock, and as the door closed with a soft hiss, he disappeared.

Ms. Grissom touched Skylar's shoulder, breaking him out of the stare he was giving the closed airlock. "Skylar, let's go to my office. We need to figure out where you're going to stay for the time being and get you into the system so the station recognizes you."

Skylar wanted to shout at her that he didn't belong there, but the numb feeling that kept him calm around Phil continued. It made him wonder what was really going on. "I thought this was a school. You make it sound like a prison camp."

She chuckled. "No, dear, I didn't mean to make it sound like that at all. We just have a few security protocols in effect to make sure everyone is safe. We train psychics here. Psychics are highly sought after in the galaxy. It's our job to make sure everyone, psychic and non-psychic, is safe." She started walking in the direction she'd come from when Skylar first spotted her.

He didn't see any choice but to follow her. "If this is a school, where are the other students?" he asked as they went through a door to the far side of the large room, and into a small office.

She walked over, sat behind a tidy desk and gestured for him to take one of the two chairs across from her. "Most of the other students are currently in class. Your arrival is actually timely, since the school day is nearly finished. I think we have just enough time to get what we need done, then I can show you where you'll be staying and see about getting you some supplies." She frowned. "From the looks of your shirt and pants, you've been wearing them for a while. Phil didn't even bother to get you clean things to put on. Sometimes Pantherians don't understand some of the basic needs that we humans have. Clothes, for instance. On their home-world, they are just as apt to go without garments. Luckily, off-world, they follow common protocol for modesty. I think our first stop will be by the MTU to get you a few outfits. We tend to be laid back around here as far as dress codes. Being open to all species makes that a necessity." She paused to tap something on her tablet.

Skylar cocked an eyebrow. "MTU?"

Ms. Grissom looked confused for a moment, then smiled tightly. "Oh, right, I doubt you had any experience with them on Hummassa. MTU is short for Mass Transformation Unit. Since we're on a space station, we try to reuse everything we can. Our non-organic waste goes into an MCU, Mass Conversion Unit, and when we need something non-organic, like clothes, equipment…whatever, we get it back, transformed by the MTUs. There are several on the station in various locations. You'll have access to the one in your dormitory wing. Since it's programmed for students, there are limits to what it will produce, but clothes and simple electronics are easy enough."

The chair Skylar had settled into was not the most comfortable. He found it easier to perch on the edge of it than lean against the hard plastic back. "So, there are a lot of other species here?"

She looked at him with a thoughtful expression. "Right now, we have twenty different species in residence. We fluctuate as folks graduate and new students arrive. Not all species have psi gifts, and some species, like Tursiops, have a higher percentage than most." She fastened a hard look on him. "You don't have any species phobias, do you?" It felt like she was staring into his mind as she did.

Skylar pursed his lips, determined to be truthful. He had no idea if she would know if he lied, or if he would be punished for it if he did. Until he had other options, he had to be honest and play along. "Boarisks."

Tapping her tablet again, Ms. Grissom nodded. "I can understand that. Luckily, they do not tend to have psychics occur naturally in their population, which is surprising considering how close to humans they really are. But, no, you won't have to worry about running into any of them in the academy. Actually, if you do run into them, please send out a general distress call at once."

He looked at her, trying to understand what she was talking about. Was he supposed to scream at the top of his lungs? "What do you mean, send out a general distress call? How do I do that?"

"We'll be fitting you with a dermal communicator," she replied without looking up from her tablet. "Once you learn to project your thoughts, all the readers in the academy will be able to hear you."

"Are you saying that I'm a reader? Is that what everyone thinks I am?" Skylar had figured out Phil had projected some kind of calming field around him as they traveled. He was a little bit surprised that his feelings were still muted unless Ms. Grissom was also doing something to him. He could hear the fit his mother would be throwing at the very idea he might have psychic powers—then, an idea hit him. If he really had psi skills, it would make it easier for him when it came time for him to begin his campaign against the Boarisks.

There was a soft chime from her tablet.

"Oh, I was waiting for this." She drew his attention back to her as she turned the tablet face up on the desk and tapped a button. A hologram of a gene sequence appeared above the tablet. "This is a display of your DNA. Notice the highlighted genes." Several of the molecules were a brilliant yellow. "Now, I can tell you're a very smart boy, even if you don't like to show it. Compare your DNA to that of another psychic gifted in two talents, like myself. You'll see that the highlighted areas are the same. Phil was able to get a sample of your mother's DNA, and there were no psi codes in her genes. This means you got your genetic traits from your father. I daresay he's a very powerful psi, but so far, we haven't been able to match your genes with any of the men in our database. The fact you don't show any non-human genes helps narrow down the search, but hasn't helped us find your family."

Skylar's mind reeled. If his father was a powerful psi, was that why his mother was always terrified of them? Had she been afraid someone might tell his father's family where he was? Did his father's family even know about him? Had she been hiding from them his whole life?

He didn't even realize Ms. Grissom had stopped talking until she cleared her throat. "I take it you might have thought of something?" When he didn't answer right away, she frowned. "Skylar, you're entering a new world here, vastly different from what you're used to. The first thing you need to understand is that, living among psychics, you shouldn't lie. The only ones you might be able to put one over on are the movers, and they aren't always as easy to fool as you would think. Now, did you think of something that might be useful in finding your extended family?"

"Mom told me that my father died in a shuttle accident about the same time as she found out that she was pregnant. He never knew about me, so I bet his family didn't either." He kept his words short and to the point.

She nodded and jotted something down on another tablet. "That might be useful. We can try to find a passenger manifest of any shuttle accidents that occurred around that time. Did your mother ever say what world the accident occurred on?"

Skylar shook his head and shifted in his seat. He hated how little he knew about his family. Teir and the other natives on Hummassa usually had large families and they knew everything about each other. The only family he had was his mother, and he felt lost and adrift without her. "No. I always assumed it was Hummassa."

"Well, it gives us a little more to get started with. Now, let's see about getting you settled. I've got your DNA in our system so the academy systems will recognize you." She stood and walked over to a panel on the wall, pulling out a small, thin, octagonal piece of metal that she gave to Skylar. "This is your dermal com chip. You can place this wherever it's comfortable. Most people put them either on the back of the hand, wrist, or under the wrist. Pantherians and some of the other furry or feathered species either have to get creative with it or get sub-dermal implants like Phil has."

Skylar took the chip, still warm from the MTU. He'd never actually seen a dermal chip before. Like the academy itself, it wasn't quite modern tech, but it was further along than what they had used on Hummassa. He held it over the back of his hand. It looked like the silver of it would stand out against his flesh. Having it on the inside of his wrist sounded better.

When Skylar put the chip against his skin, it burned slightly as it melded to him. *Wow!* But he tried not to show a reaction in front of the counselor. A strange warmth flowed up his arm, and he realized that, even if it was an older tech, there was still a nano-component to it as something buzzed in his ear for a moment, as the com made a connection to his auditory nerve. He tugged at his earlobe, but the buzzing died away quickly.

Ms. Grissom looked at his wrist and nodded. "Your body seems to be accepting it okay. We haven't had a human reject a com chip in many years. Now, let's get you some clothes, find your room, and with luck, you'll be in the common room in time for the other students to get there before dinner." She started for the door before he could get out of his seat.

Skylar rushed to follow her. It was the first time he'd been on a space station. He wanted to make sure he didn't miss anything important. It didn't hurt that the idea of seeing more of the station gave him the opportunity to stop thinking about the fact he had psychic DNA and his father had probably been a powerful psychic.

6
Explosion In The Restroom

BY THE time they returned to the common room, Skylar's head was abuzz with all the things Ms. Grissom had shown him. She assigned him a bunk in one of the dorm rooms that, she assured him, had people he would be able to get along with. She let him select several changes of clothes from the MTU in the hall near his room, and after he had the clothes stashed, she gave him a whirlwind tour of what she referred to as the 'human living areas.' There were no airlocks or warnings like there were on two halls off the entry room. On the walls just outside those hazardous areas, there were life support suits in the rare case he might need to go in there. The classrooms were in the human zone with an oxygen-rich atmosphere, and she explained the non-oxygen breathers had to use their species-specific life-support there too, as well as in the farm and green areas, which were in the large open place he and Phil had flown over. It looked even larger and greener inside. The air smelled almost like Hummassa and gave him a pang of homesickness. After too quick a tour, she brought him back to the entry room.

Ms. Grissom's tablet beeped. She took a quick look at it. "Oh, dear. Skylar, you'll need to excuse me for a while. I completely forgot an important meeting in the principal's office. I'm sure you can handle things from here on out. I've given you the same schedule as your dorm mates, so just go with them tomorrow as they attend their classes. Your com can help you find your way around." Her tablet beeped again.

"I think I'll be fine," Skylar reassured her. He wanted her to leave so he could sort out his thoughts. Everything was happening fast and he hadn't had time to digest it. "If not, I know where your office is." He really hoped he didn't need to go into her office very often.

She nodded. "Check in with me tomorrow before dinner and let me know how your first day goes."

As she disappeared into a door not far from her office, Skylar took a long, deep breath. *Alone.* He glanced around. There still weren't students in the common room.

He walked over to one of the large displays that showed a real-time image of the massive orange gas giant, that appeared to be the planet between the station and the sun. The bright clouds swirled erratically. One of the planet's moons appeared from behind its bulk and slowly started its way across the brilliant spectacle.

Skylar's life had changed so much in such a short time. He wondered where Teir was. The last Phil checked, he was still among the missing. At least, not knowing, he could imagine Teir was still alive somewhere, unlike his mother. For a moment, a sadness welled up in him, then vanished, like it had never been there. It didn't make any sense how his emotions would start to react to something, then just fade away.

"Hey, out of my way!" a boy shouted from behind Skylar. "I've got to go before dinner, and I'm not going to be late. They're serving Regilian enchiladas tonight."

Skylar turned as students swarmed out of the classroom area. True to Ms. Grissom's word, there was a wide variety of species represented. He spotted several Pantherians, along with a couple of Tursiops, their smooth gray skin evolved from an aquatic environment. They were lucky they were also mammalian-based and oxygen breathers. There was a huge mollusk of a race he remembered seeing pictures of, but the name eluded him. An avian ran past, then an amoeboid, encased in a life chamber that floated about and allowed it to exist outside of the non-oxygen atmosphere that normally sustained it. Skylar tried not to stare, but the mix was so different from what he was used to on Hummassa. Even though corp-brats could come from any planet, all the ones he was used to being ignored by were the humanoid type.

Joining the rush of people heading toward the cafeteria, Skylar's bladder pressure reminded him he hadn't been to the bathroom since he'd woken up on Phil's ship. He glanced for the boy who'd shouted, but couldn't see him in the people streaming through the room.

Several kids broke off from the flow and disappeared through a door with a toilet-shaped graphic indicating bathroom. Inside, the midsized room was packed with kids of various ages, most of them already disappeared into stalls. A few were already at sinks.

One human boy with long black hair looked at Skylar as he held his hands in the stream of air emanating from a jet next to the door. "Hey, if you've really got to go, use that blue door at the end. It's a multispecies stall. It'll be okay."

Skylar looked at the boy. An odd feeling of mischief from the kid hit him, but he really needed to go. "Thanks." He hurried down to the blue door. When he closed it, it sealed like an air lock. There was a thick sulfur smell, and the stool at the far end extended out further than normal and was pointed at the end. He glanced at it. It was still brightly polished metal with a series of holes in it.

Shifting from foot to foot, he couldn't deny his urgency and longer. It didn't matter if the thing was a little odd shaped.

A minute later, as he zipped up his pants, smoke began to issue from the stool. "What in the world?" Skylar pushed against the door, but it wouldn't open. The smoke got thicker. He turned the handle. It turned and there was a hiss of an opening seal, but the door still wouldn't open. It felt like there was someone holding it shut. The smoke intensified and started burning his nose.

Skylar slammed his shoulder against the door. It jumped slightly but didn't open. A series of laughs came from the other side.

"Let me out of here, you jerks!"

"That's enough!" someone shouted on the other side of the door. "Let him out!"

"Or what, fish brain? You going to make us?" threatened the kid who'd told him to use the blue door in the first place.

The toilet creaked and a loud gurgling started. It sounded like it was about to erupt. Skylar hit the door with all his might. The door flew open and he sprawled across the threshold, just as the urinal exploded off the wall and hurled over him.

The kid with the long black hair stood there laughing, as did two others. "I think that's the furthest that thing has ever flown before. You must've really had to go." He turned and gestured to his friends. "Come on, I don't want to miss dinner."

On the other side of the door stood a short Tursiops with short, light-blue hair. He offered Skylar a hand up. "Don't mind them. They're corp-brats who think they're better than the rest of us. We're not all like that around here."

Skylar accepted the hand up. A rush of shared compassion hit him, then passed. The boy's webbed fingers felt strange. Even though his skin looked like it should be rubbery, it was actually fairly soft. "Thanks. I've dealt with guys like that before. I'm Skylar."

"Del. So you're the new kid Ms. Grissom told me to expect. Blue 19, right?"

"Yeah. Is that your room too?" Ms. Grissom had told him he should get along with his roommates. So far, Del had tried to rescue him from the exploding toilet. That was a good start. If he kept doing things like that, Skylar would be happy to make friends with him.

Del nodded. "Yep. I'll introduce you to the others after supper." A feeling of loneliness hit Skylar as Del continued, "They tend to eat with some of their other friends. But hey, I can help you learn the ropes, since Ms. Grissom said you were going to be on the same schedule as the rest of us. That is, if you don't mind following me around until you get the hang of everything here. Some folks say I go on a bit too much."

Skylar couldn't help but smile. He felt he was on the way to making his first friend in his new school. Even if he didn't know how long he was going to be there, it felt good to get to know someone. "Sure, I'm good with following you around."

The bathroom door clanged open and a three-foot-tall cleaning bot entered.

"Come on, we better get out of its way," Del said, motioning for Skylar to leave the now-empty restroom. "Last week, somebody failed to move fast enough and ended up getting a good scrubbing."

"I've never actually seen a cleaning bot work," Skylar said. "I mean, I've seen vids and read about them, but this is the first one I've seen. That is unless you count the remote controlled jack bot the Intergal Rescue gal had."

Del stopped in the doorway and seemed to study Skylar. "Where are you from that you've never seen a cleaning bot in action before? I thought they were everywhere."

"I'm from Hummassa. It's a little backwater spot out on the edge of settled space. We were a little behind times." He hoped the feeling of being a hick disappeared as he looked back over his shoulder at the cleaning bot which had started removing the wreckage. It might be something that was everyday for Del, but for Skylar, it was totally new and interesting.

"Must've been." Del led Skylar in the direction of the flow of students had been moving earlier. The common room was once again clear. "We might not have all the most modern tech around here, but we're a bit beyond *that*. I guess you're going to have a bit of a learning curve here, like not using the Vi-Go-Tions' stalls."

"Was that what happened?"

"Yeah, their fluids don't mix well with ours. The results can be volatile. As you now know. Pathal and his gang like to trick the new kids into using the blue stalls and watch them explode. You got lucky. One of the kids they did it to caught the urinal in his back and spent a day in the med bay getting patched up. That poor kid still walks funny and never uses the public toilets. Can't say as I blame him."

"I guess I'm lucky you came along when you did." Skylar relaxed as they strolled through the archway that opened into the cafeteria. His thoughts eased up more than they had since waking up in the jungle. He didn't even mind that a lot of heads turned his way. He'd survived the corp-brats' first attempt. With Del around to show him the ropes, he didn't doubt he would survive the next round too.

7
Meeting A Mover

UNTIL HIS head hit the pillow, Skylar hadn't realized how tired he was. He fell into a quick but restless sleep. His dreams were filled with visions of his mother, the raider's bombardment of Hummassa, and exploding toilets. The tall, dark man also made an appearance. Again, something inhuman screamed in the distance; it sounded like it was in distress, or at the very least angry about something.

Waking a little before the alarm sounded, Skylar lay in bed sweating even though the temperature in the room was set to be comfortable for humans and Tursiops. He finally decided to get up as quietly as possible and grab his shower before Del and his other two roommates woke up.

By the time he emerged from the bathroom, the other three were waiting for him.

Connor, the other human in the room, glared at him. "We're all on a schedule here. If you make us all late for breakfast, I'll remember it for as long as you're here." He shoved past Skylar and slammed the bathroom door.

Del shook his head. "Don't mind him. He's just a little grumpy in the morning. I'm really hoping that's not a human trait, although I haven't noticed it in all the humans here, just a few."

Fin, another Tursiops, shrugged and said in a low voice, "I don't really think his folks taught him much in the way of manners. He's not as bad as some of the corp-kids around here, but he still doesn't cast you humans in the best light. If you know what I mean."

"Yeah, I know what you mean." Having dealt with a fair number of corp-brats back on Hummassa, Skylar knew the type all too well. After Pathal and the toilet the previous evening, and now Connor, he was beginning to wonder if all the humans at Stars' End were jerks. Del and Fin appeared dressed as they had been the previous evening, in sleek, gray synthetic jumpsuits that looked similar. "Aren't you two waiting for the shower too?"

"Nope," Del said, "most Tursiops bathe before sleep. Immersion in water helps us relax. Plus, showers are a bit harsh on our skin. We were just about to head down to the cafeteria for some breakfast. If we get out fast enough, we can lose Connor for a bit and he'll wake up and be a little more cordial."

"Yeah, right," Fin sniped.

Skylar tossed his toiletries on his bunk—the one above where Del slept—and gestured to the door. "Let's get going then."

Del held the door as the other two walked into the simple beige hall. There were already a fair number of students and staff moving around, and most everyone headed toward the common room and cafeteria.

"I got to thinking about it." Del continued along with Skylar while Fin stopped to talk to another Tursiops. "Our semester just started about two weeks ago. You have good timing, showing up when you did. With any luck, you won't have a lot of catch up to do. But if you do, I'll be happy to help you. I can get you through everything we've done so far without too much trouble. That is, if you want me to."

That was something that Skylar hadn't given any thought to. What if they were a lot further along in things than his school back home? And would there be classes on things that his mom would've had a fit over, like psychic skills? It was a school for psychics—surely some of his lessons would be about that, particularly since they said he had psychic DNA. "My school was destroyed in the raider's attack. I don't know if any files remain that could be transferred. That might cause trouble."

Del shook his head. "Probably not. I bet while you were talking to her yesterday, Ms. Grissom did a full assessment without you even realizing it. If she didn't, she probably had Grandfather do it. She's always asking him to probe people while she's talking to them. It's not exactly ethical, but technically we're all minors, so although we have to obey the laws, they don't exactly apply to us the same way as they will depending on our job choices. Counselors like Ms. Grissom, teachers and such are given a bit more leeway than some."

Although he had other questions, one thing stood out for him. Skylar stopped and looked at Del. "Your grandfather is here?"

"Yeah." Del nodded. "That's one of the reasons I'm here." He frowned a bit. "Grandfather Aduncus is the head reader teacher. He's a level-ten reader. I'm just a lowly level two feeler. Lowest ranking psi my family has produced in generations. Luckily I've got the highest IQ ever seen in my family. I can remember almost everything I've ever read or seen and can make use of the knowledge without any strain. But it would be nice to rank a little higher on the psi scales."

"Wow, that's cool! Not that you rank low, but that you're so smart. I'm used to being smart too…okay, a bit average in school work, but at least the math and stuff makes sense," Skylar said. "But you think your grandfather was probing my brain if Ms. Grissom wasn't? That's creepy."

He didn't bother adding that he wanted to learn how to keep other people out of his head and away from his thoughts as soon as he could. First, Phil played with his emotions, then people were reading his mind without permission. It wasn't polite. He understood some of his mother's fears about being around psychics, but he pushed those concerns back. If he had skills, he wanted to learn how to use them so they could be useful in the future.

Del shrugged and they started walking again. "You're just getting started at school. They rationalize the mental invasion as an attempt to figure out what you're all about, and that it was the best thing for you. And like I said, you're underage at this point."

Skylar sighed as they entered the common room. "I love the way that adults can always rationalize the things they do to us. It's like Phil taking my anger away from me and making me want to come with him."

"Yeah." Del nodded emphatically. "Exactly! Sometimes they think it's okay just to make us into their own personal puppets. But hey, now you're here, at least until they find your family, right? If you test strong enough, they might try to convince your family to let you stay. That'd be good." A feeling of hope poured out of Del, making Skylar wonder if he was lonely in the midst of the others in the school. Maybe ranking low on the psychic scales left him picked on. Although the only ones who'd bullied Skylar back home were the corp-brats, he didn't like the idea that someone would pick on Del. They needed to stick together for that reason alone.

Skylar watched the common room fill up as they waited for the doors to the cafeteria to open. There was a wider variety of species than he'd ever hoped to meet— he wondered where some of them had been the previous evening. They were in the middle of space, even if the artificial gravity of the station did make it feel like they were on a planet.

He smiled at Del. "Yeah, I think maybe that would be good." Even if it meant embracing part of himself that he'd never known he had, and that his mom had feared.

DEL RUSHED down the hall as the number of students dwindled. "Come on, Skylar. We don't want to be late for your first class. It'll make a bad impression."

Skylar hurried along in his wake. "Sorry." They'd been talking with some of the other students as they ate their breakfast and lost track of time. It was nice to discover he was going to have a few things in common with his classmates. There was discussion of various games, complaining about teachers, new net sites folks had visited—all in all, it sounded like most of his school lunches had back on Hummassa. Del had actually done most of the talking, but the others seemed nice and welcoming.

"It's your first full day. I'll forgive you this time." Del grinned mischievously and turned into the last door on the hallway.

Skylar skidded to a stop behind him. The room looked nearly identical to his classroom on Hummassa. All the students had individual workstations with dual monitors. The chairs looked just as uncomfortable as what he was used to. For a second, the normalcy of it put him at ease.

"Please take your seats," the teacher, a tall, red-haired human barked without looking up from his terminal.

"Where?" Skylar asked. The class was nearly full and he had no idea where he should sit.

Del shrugged as he started toward two seats on the far side of the room. Skylar followed.

As they sat down, Skylar clicked on his station. It worked just like the ones he was used to, even if the colors were a bit more vivid and it booted faster. "I don't see any other open stations."

"There is someone who normally sits there." Del's webbed fingers flew across his lower monitor, and he didn't look up. "A blue kid from Cephylon. But I don't see him right now. His name is something most of us have trouble pronouncing, so we just gave up trying. Everyone calls him Si'lop. You'll find that a lot of the kids with odd names end up with nicknames. It's easier."

A second later, Skylar looked up to see a blue kid run into class and stop halfway across the room. He looked at Skylar and raised a green eyebrow.

"Why can't any of you take your seats like you're supposed to?" the teacher demanded. "There is still one of you out of a seat. Get into your workstation so we can begin."

The blue kid heaved a sigh, then hurried over to the only other open desk. It was on the far side of the classroom. As soon as he sat, the teacher stood.

"Very good. I was starting to think that class was never going to start today." He clicked something, the lights dimmed, and a hologram appeared in the middle of the room as he started in about simple physics.

About ten minutes into class, something flashed on the far side of the room. At the same time, a loud pop broke the teacher's boring lecture.

The teacher looked up from his monitor and scanned the room. "Okay, who's the wise guy?"

His gaze lingered on the blue student. "Si'Lop. What are you doing over there?"

Before the kid could answer, another flash lit up the same area as the first. A loud boom shook the room.

From the workstation next to Skylar's, Del unsuccessfully tried to muffle a guffaw. Skylar looked at him. "What?" he whispered.

A pronounced fart sounded, followed by another flash that brightened everything before the loudest boom yet rolled across the space.

The blue kid got up and walked toward the teacher as other students chuckled and laughed softly. "I'm sorry, sir. My regular seat was occupied when I got here. You said I needed to get in a chair and the only one available was near the heating unit."

The teacher looked at Skylar, then at Del. "Aduncus, was this your idea? You put poor Si'Lop out of his seat just to disrupt class?"

Del shook his head. "No, sir. It was an honest mistake."

More of the class laughed.

Skylar stood up. "I'm sorry, sir. I didn't realize my taking a seat would cause a problem." He looked at Si'Lop. "Have your seat back. I'll take the other one." He walked toward the front of the room.

Si'Lop nodded slightly. It caused his green hair to drop down in front of his brilliant ruby-red eyes. "It's not a problem, this time."

I've got a lot to learn about other species, Skylar thought as he walked to his new seat. *First exploding toilets and now flashing farts. What's next? Flaming crap?*

STIFLING A yawn with his hand, Skylar struggled to pay attention to the teacher at the head of the class. Professor Corda was the first Cryptod Skylar had ever met. Del explained before class that the slight hunch in the teacher's back was actually a vestigial shell. Professor Corda was one of the non-psychics on the teaching staff, but he was over seven hundred years old. Before class started, the human girl sitting in front of them said he was one of the original Cryptods and may have actually been around at the start of the Central Galactic Council, which was only nine hundred years old.

So far, most of the class was stuff Skylar already knew. Combined with the fact that Professor Corda had a very dry, unchanging voice, it was enough to make him drift off. Even trying to focus on the various historic holograms around the room didn't help as the Cryptod droned on about how humans had expanded out into the galaxy and used both terraforming and gene manipulation to make worlds and humans more adaptable and usable.

Something nudged his ill-repaired ear.

Skylar turned and looked over his shoulder. The desk behind him was empty. He glanced across the aisle at Del, but his friend appeared entranced by their teacher.

When Skylar turned his attention to the hologram that Professor Corda pointed to, someone flicked his hair. It was the barest of touches, this time on the other side of his head. In that direction floated one of the cephalopod students in its containment bubble. Skylar didn't see any way it could've touched him. It turned one of its eyestalks toward him and blinked. Skylar raised his hand, trying to gesture that he wasn't trying to draw the cephalopod's attention.

"Our newest student, Mr. Mars, has a question," Professor Corda said.

The blood drained from Skylar's face. He didn't have a question. He gulped as he tried to find something to say that wouldn't sound stupid. "Have sentient species been engineered, and which gene combination worked the best?"

What could've been a frown crossed the teacher's scaly face—it was hard to tell since he looked like he had a constant frown. "Mr. Mars, that's actually a much more appropriate question to ask in the interplanetary biology class, but since you ask, at last count, there are only three species still around that are a result of various gene splicing strategies that have since been outlawed. Many of us longer-lived lifeforms find what your species has done in the past incredible, but there are others who feel the technology was not human in origin, but something left over from the originators of life itself. As a teacher, I try not to let personal opinion cloud my ability to teach. If you don't have any other questions, I'd like to continue my lecture."

Skylar shook his head. "No, that was all. Thank you." He wished he could dissolve into his chair and never set foot in the classroom again. He hated it when he inadvertently drew attention to himself. It always caused trouble, and he'd hoped to avoid that.

"You are most welcome. *I* wouldn't want to make a bad impression on your first day." The teacher turned back to his hologram and continued his lecture.

A soft giggle came from behind Skylar. He wanted to turn and look but was afraid of attracting the teacher's attention. For the rest of the class, the invisible flicking of his ears and hair continued.

When the rest of his classmates started for the door as the tone signaling the end of class sounded, Skylar spun around and caught the gaze of the Pantherian girl sitting three rows back. There hadn't been anybody sitting between them, and she had a mischievous gleam in her ice blue eyes.

Skylar stood and strolled back to her. "Are you that one who's been flicking me?" He tried to sound serious without sounding overly confrontational. Most people knew better than to antagonize a Pantherian. They weren't known for their calm demeanors and tended to fly off the handle at the least little provocation.

She shrugged and yawned, exposing her fangs. "Maybe. What's with your ear anyway? A bad gene splice?"

"No." He glared.

Standing, she stretched. Her thick mane of gray and white hair fluffed out. It started along her back and worked its way outward. Shaking her head, she cracked her neck, and finally extended her claws and shook her hands. A huge smile crossed her white furry face that made her silver whiskers lift. "Good. I thought you were pure human. Just deformed then. Well, I've got to get to my next class."

The other students and the teacher had all left the room. Del waited near the door. Skylar touched her arm as she started past him "So you spent nearly an hour flicking my ear just so you could ask me about it? And how were you doing that?"

She arched a light gray eyebrow as she looked down at him. "You are new to this whole psi thing, aren't you? I'm a mover. That means I move things with my thoughts." She jerked her arm out of his grasp with a flash of fang. "Now, if you don't mind, I've got a class to get to." With a swish of her long, mottled white and gray hair, she stomped past Del and out of the room.

"She's not really someone you want to upset," Del said as Skylar walked up to him. "You know Pantherians are notoriously high-strung and unpredictable. There aren't many species who can compete with them in the dangerous department."

"I've only met one. Phil, the one who brought me here." Skylar started walking down the hall, not waiting for Del to lead them to their next class.

"Well, now you've met two." Del dropped his voice. "I bet Solaria isn't anything like Phil. First, she's female."

"I kinda noticed that." Skylar wondered if the females were more dangerous than the males. He knew in a lot of societies that was true.

"She's also a mover. Rumor has it she's not very strong, but there's not a lot of movers out there, so there are already recruiters looking to place her in one of the corporations. Movers are in very high demand." Del stopped near a door and gestured that they should enter. "Just be careful around her."

Solaria sat in the back of the new classroom. Skylar looked at the only two empty desks in the room—they were next to her. "Guess we get to see if we can make friends." Even if his feelings had been manipulated by Phil, he had still liked the Pantherian feeler. There was something about Pantherians that made him think he should try and be friendly to her. At least if they were friends, she'd be less likely to eat him.

Del sighed as he headed for the desk farthest from Solaria. "Tell you what, if she squashes you in the hall, I'll pick up the pieces and get you to the med bay. It might take a while for the swelling to go down though."

Skylar chuckled. "She's not going to squash me." He took the seat next to her. "Looks like we've got at least two classes together. I didn't mean to sound grumpy about the flicking thing. Like you said, I'm new to this 'whole psychic thing.' I guess you get to break me in."

A feral, predatory grin crossed her face and her fangs flashed again. "It's almost like you just gave me permission, human."

He offered her a friendly hand. "I'm Skylar. I just found out I'm a psychic. I was actually brought to the station by a Pantherian named Philaneo Clawson. He was cool."

Her look softened as her hand curled around his. Her claws pricked the back of his hand. "Solaria. So, you're the reason Uncle Phil stopped by but couldn't stay. Ms. Grissom didn't give me any details."

"Phil's your uncle? But you two don't look anything alike." As the words left his mouth, Skylar kicked himself for fear that he may have just alienated her. He was always good at putting his foot in his mouth.

She sighed as she released his hand. "My mom is his half-sister on their sire's side. I look more like my sire than my mother. So where did Uncle Phil find you?"

"Hummassa, after a Boarisk raid. They killed my mother and all my friends are missing or dead. Phil helped me deal with it." For the first time, Skylar started to see that maybe Phil's manipulation had been more for his own good than just yanking him around by his emotions. Even if people didn't like not having constant control of themselves, psychic manipulation might be able to be used for good, under certain circumstances.

"He's a level ten feeler. He's good at that." She dropped her voice as the teacher, a human, came into the room. "Look, if Uncle Phil brought you to the academy, then you must be okay. I'll cut you some slack, I suppose. But get out of line, human, and I *will* rip you apart. But, then again, my uncle would probably appreciate me keeping an eye on you." She pursed her lips and slowly inclined her head. "You could be interesting. Predators hate when things—or people—get boring."

Skylar nodded. Not the best start to a new friendship, but it was a first step. He'd had worse over the years. "Thanks."

The teacher called the class to order and all talking stopped. Skylar found it a little easier to stay awake and pay attention as he got his first formal explanations of psychic morals and responsibilities. There was a lot more to it than he'd expected. Like Del had said, there were standards for different types of psychics. Readers were held to a very high standard, expected to only use their abilities to the benefit of those around them, and never for selfish reasons. Since they could be the most intrusive, they were considered the most dangerous. Feelers were given a bit more freedom, but they could still directly influence people, as Skylar well knew, but again, it was supposed to be for the person's own good. Movers were deemed the least likely to be personally invasive and didn't have the strict monitoring the other two did. He'd been amazed to find out that some really strong movers could teleport themselves from place to place. It was extremely rare in an already small group of people.

The thing that surprised him the most was that each skill had its own form of licensing a user had to undergo before the psychic could lawfully use their powers. Unlicensed psis were a constant problem for the Central Galactic Council, and there were special people to deal with them. Hunters. These were barely touched on, and Skylar wanted to know more.

With a new friend on either side of him, Skylar felt ready for the challenges of the class and life in the academy. With Del's brains and Solaria's brawn, he figured he'd be just fine. The questions that arose in him were what was going to happen to him after school, and just where was he going to fit into the galaxy.

Chapter 8
What Is Skylar?

JERKING AWAKE had become a common thing, and it was something Skylar wished would go away. Every night he relived the fire and his mother's death. In his dreams, he kept hearing screams like he'd never heard before from a creature, or something. He never actually saw a screaming creature, so he had no idea what it was. Then there was the dark man who never moved out of the shadows, never came into focus. As he looked at the ceiling waiting for his heartbeat to stop racing, he was just thankful he hadn't woken up Del, Connor, or Fin. That would've been more embarrassment than he wanted to deal with.

Like he'd done the previous two mornings, he slipped out of bed and hit the shower before the others woke up. The water helped him clear his head and get ready for the day. There was so much new and strange information coming at him every day he hadn't been bored—well outside of history class. That was the same no matter where he went, although history at Stars' End included psychics' roles, where those had been neglected at the school on Hummassa.

As he walked back into the main dorm room, there was a slight buzzing in his head. He glanced at his dermal com. The name 'Philaneo Clawson' glowed just above his skin. It was his first communication from someone outside the school—although when he stopped to think about it, he didn't really know anyone other than Phil off the station. Everyone else was either dead or missing.

Skylar tapped the com to activate the call. The glowing name was replaced by Phil's image. "Hi, Skylar. I hope I got the time difference right and you're awake."

"Nightmares." Skylar shrugged. "I get up early."

Phil frowned. "With everything you went through, that's perfectly understandable. If you decide you need to talk to anyone about it, I'm sure Fiona…ah, Ms. Grissom will be happy to listen."

Skylar shook his head. "Probably not." He really didn't want to spend a lot of time around Ms. Grissom.

"Okay. Unfortunately, I call bearing bad news. We've finished locating the survivors of the attack. I had time to go check your home." Phil looked down and sighed. "Your house was destroyed in the fire that ravaged the jungle around it. I'm still amazed you survived unburned."

"So, there was nothing." Skylar's heart sank. Even though he was getting used to receiving bad news on a regular basis, it still hurt.

Phil brightened slightly. "I didn't say that. I took a little while to dig through the rubble and see if I could salvage anything." He held up a small locket and a matching ring.

They were pieces his mother had kept in a small jewelry box in her bedroom. She wasn't big on any kind of personal adornment, so she didn't wear them much, just on really special occasions. She'd told him they were pieces her mother had left her and had been handed down in the family for generations. Skylar's throat tightened, and he pursed his lips to keep them from trembling. "They were Mom's."

"I figured. I'll keep them with me and bring them to you the next time I drop by to see you and Solaria. You've met my niece, haven't you?"

Skylar welcomed the change of subject. "Yes, she's taking some getting used to, but she's nice."

Phil laughed. "She better be, or I'll scruff her hard."

Skylar tried to envision anyone, even Phil, picking Solaria up by the scruff of her neck. It made him smile.

Before he could say anything, his com buzzed in his ear. A soft electronic voice said, "Ms. Grissom."

"Phil, Ms. Grissom is calling. I need to take this, but before I get off here, anything about Teir or his family?"

Phil shook his head again. "I'm sorry, they're on the officially missing list. I wish I had better news. You better take Ms. Grissom's call."

"Thanks." Skylar tapped his com to change calls.

"Are you finished sleeping, Mr. Mars?" Ms. Grissom started talking before the holographic image of her appeared over Skylar's wrist.

"Phil connected with me right before you tried to. Sorry about that." He wasn't really sorry, and he hoped the distance between them kept her from reading his mind.

She waved off his comment. "I didn't have to come get you, so you're okay. I need you to report to my office this morning."

Skylar's heart sank. He hadn't even been in school a week and he was already being called into the office. "What time?"

"As soon as possible." Ms. Grissom glanced at something Skylar couldn't see with the limited view the hologram gave him. "I've already informed your teachers you'll miss your morning classes. You should be finished by lunch. I'll see you shortly." She disconnected before he could respond.

"I bet you're going to get tested," Del said from where he was sitting on the edge of his bunk, the one under Skylar's.

Skylar frowned. "Tested?"

Fin chuckled as he pulled on his blue tunic and finished getting dressed for the day. "You really don't know much about being a psychic."

Del softly kicked Fin in the butt. "Be nice—you know he didn't grow up the same way we did." He looked at Skylar. "Every psi gets tested, most of us when we're in our early teens, or before. You're a little late, but we already knew that. Don't worry. It's not like she's going to shove electrified needles into you and see how you jump. It's fairly simple. But she knows you're already dressed, so you better go get some breakfast and get to her office. If anyone asks, I'll let them know. Honestly, I figured this would've happened either your first day, or yesterday."

Tested for psi skills. Skylar took a quick look in the mirror and adjusted his hair that was still a little spikey from his shower. His mother would hate him being tested for psi skills, particularly after what Ms. Grissom had said about him having gene markers. He wasn't sure if he wanted to know what he could do or not.

SKYLAR WATIED for Ms. Grissom to answer her door. He shifted from foot to foot and wished his brown jumpsuit had pockets. Then he could've stuck his hands in them, or at least found something to do with them.

The door opened and his heart pounded like crazy.

"Ah, Skylar." Ms. Grissom came out to meet him. "I thought I heard you out here. Come along. I've got the testing room set up."

"There's a special room for testing?" He wasn't sure what to expect, other than Del said it wouldn't be painful.

She nodded as she led him down the hall toward the classrooms. "Yes. It's specially shielded to keep anything that might arise down to a minimum impact on the other students."

Her phrasing didn't calm him any. He couldn't imagine what kind of things would arise from simply testing him for talent that would affect his classmates.

They walked past the classrooms, and then she turned down a hallway that Skylar had never taken before. It was the other way from the locker rooms and gym located at the far end of the education halls. Then she stopped at a panel and tapped a code into the lock. The door slid open and she waved him into the room.

There were a series of screens on the far wall where empty graphs appeared to be waiting for input of some kind. A large cushioned chair sat in the middle of the room with a bright light above it. A couple of smaller chairs were at different spots around the room.

"Please take a seat in the chair," Ms. Grissom directed him. "And try not to be nervous. I need you to relax for me to get proper readings."

Skylar settled himself into the chair. It was cold and felt like it was engulfing him. "I'll do my best."

"Thank you." She went over to one of the panels. "Maybe it will help if I do some explaining while the sensors start doing their work. Do you have any questions?"

"About what?" Skylar knew she was trying to put him at ease, but sitting there in the chair was one of the more awkward things he'd done lately. There was something about the quiet room with all the screens that felt odd, and almost dangerous.

"I know your teachers have explained some of the aspects of being a psychic to you. They probably left you with more than a few questions, unless Del has been so good as to bring you up to speed." She tapped the panel in front of her and it brightened.

Skylar didn't want to tell her that Del had told him a lot more than his teachers had. "I'm not exactly sure how the various skills are ranked. I know Phil is a level 10 feeler, but I don't know what that means, other than it has to do with how strong he is." Del had tried to explain things to Skylar, but like a lot of the other smart kids he'd known, Del got too complicated and it had gone over his head.

Ms. Grissom walked over to another panel and tapped it. "A good place to start. Also, a fairly complex subject. The levels are a little different for each skill, although feeler and reader levels are fairly similar. For them it's an indication of either their range or how many people they can influence. The lower the level, the less range and fewer people. Also, the less complex things they can pick up or project."

"Del says he's a level two feeler, so that means he can't pick up a whole lot."

"That's right." Ms. Grissom stared at one of the panels and shook her head. "I doubt Del could really influence another person's emotions very much. Level twos just don't have it in them."

"Can levels change?" Del had made it sound like psi skills were a bit like muscles, and could be strengthened with time and practice.

"All the time, but your base gives us an idea of what you're capable of. Think about how some people have the physical build to be extremely strong. You can't expect a really skinny person to ever be able to lift several hundred kilos even with a lot of training—they just don't have the bone structure to handle the muscle stress of it. This is a lot like that." She did something on the screen in front of her. The lights in the room dimmed slightly and the chair vibrated around him.

The sudden motion startled him and he jumped slightly, looking down at the chair and hoping it wouldn't do that anymore.

"Sorry. Got to get things warmed up." The counselor moved on, to the only panel she hadn't stopped at yet. "But anyway, that's what we're going to do today. We're going to see if I can figure out which gifts you're gene-active for and what level you have." A spiral helix appeared on the screen in front of her. "It took me a little while to study your DNA, and it's interesting that you have markers for every known skill. That's extremely unusual in someone who doesn't have any non-human markers. If I had to guess, I'd say your father is a very powerful psychic with multiple active genes, but without knowing who he is, we can't be sure."

She was frowning when she turned away from the screen. "Every time I try and track anything down, I hit a datablock. I've got our IT department working on getting past them, but someone in your family doesn't want to be identified. With so many of the big corp families using illegal gene splicing on themselves and their offspring, it makes it difficult to accurately track families. I'm trying to look beyond your psi genes and find basic traits I can track."

Skylar knew enough about what she was saying to understand that she was trying to look into things like his blood type, skin and hair color and other things that made him human, and find the family he belonged to. He also understood that would be difficult since a lot of people, particularly wealthy corporate types, tended to use illegal gene splicing techniques to make themselves and their children the best, the prettiest, the strongest they could be. It wasn't a search he deemed worthwhile, but if she wanted to adopt his parentage as her pet project he wouldn't worry about it.

A gentle electric current went through him. He sat a little straighter in the chair. "I thought Del said there wasn't going to be any electrified needles."

"An electric field helps us know what's active and what's not," Ms. Grissom said as she went back to the middle panel. "It's low level enough that it shouldn't hurt humans."

"What about non-humans?" He wondered if some species were tortured to see if they had any powers.

"We have other techniques for the ones who are overly sensitive to electricity." She made an adjustment on the panel. "This is odd."

"What?" Skylar leaned forward, then felt like he hit a force field. "Hey."

Ms. Grissom made a dismissive gesture. "You're safe. Don't worry about that." She stared at the screen in front of her. "We knew you were a strong feeler. Level five is a good starting point. You'll never reach level ten, can go a few more levels with practice, but based on your genes, there should be more."

Skylar did his best to not freak out in the chair. He kept telling himself that Phil wouldn't have taken him somewhere he could get hurt or worse. Although he'd been emotionally manipulated at the time, he still felt Phil had his best interest at heart. Talking helped him stay calm. "If you're basing so much off my genes, then why can't they show you what's active and what's recessive?"

"Because psi genes don't exactly work like other genes," she replied. "Sometimes they need the right stimulation to become active. It looked like you've become emotionally active, but nothing else." She stepped away from the panel. *"It's amazing that there's nothing else active."* Her voice rang out in his mind and something pulled at him.

Was she was trying to do something to make another gene activate. "What makes a gene activate then? You make it sound like it's some kind of electrical circuit."

"In many ways, it is. There are a good number of documented cases where a gene didn't become active until it was needed." She walked over to the first panel and tapped something.

The humming in the chair stopped and Skylar relaxed a little bit. He didn't try the force field, but waited for Ms. Grissom to continue.

"More than a few movers activate when something is falling toward them, or readers when they are trying to reach out to a lost loved one. Adrenaline is very useful in activating genes." She took out a set of virtual reality goggles and gloves that looked like a newer version of the ones Skylar had used when gaming with Teir. "Unfortunately, it's not acceptable to put people into real-life dangerous situations."

She handed the rig to Skylar. "These simulations are the best we can do."

"What kind of simulations are there?" He felt a lot calmer once it appeared Del was right and he wasn't going to get poked. VR, he could deal with.

"A couple of different ones." Ms. Grissom walked back to the panels as he put the goggles and gloves on. "I'll set up the first one."

The goggles came to life and Skylar found himself standing on the edge of a cliff. A swarm of Belsomic Honey Bees flew at him. He ducked and envisioned a glowing shield in front of him. The simulation was close enough to Galactic Explorers that it responded the same way and the giant red bees bounced off the shield.

For the next hour, several similar scenarios played out. He wasn't sure if he was supposed to be using his gaming knowledge to protect himself or not, but it made sense to use what he knew to stay alive, or at least keep his avatar alive, so he dodged rockslides, flew over lava pits and blasted slavers until Ms. Grissom ended the simulation. Being immersed in VR was the most fun he'd had since being at Stars' End.

As she took the VR rig from him, Ms. Grissom was shaking her head. "It really doesn't make any sense. You should be more than just a feeler, but that's all that's active."

"But that can change depending on my situation?" Skylar wanted to ask to keep the VR, but hadn't been told about the academy's regulations on gaming, if it was even allowed.

"That's right." She put the VR equipment in the storage cabinet between two of the panels. "Don't worry, we'll keep an eye on you. Regardless of anything else showing up or not, we'll need to teach you to shield, to block out the thoughts and feelings of others and to keep them out of your mind. Most of our students learn shielding before anything else. I'll decide which teacher would be best to teach you that skill."

If it meant he could learn to protect his thoughts from the prying minds of people like Ms. Grissom, Skylar wanted to start those lessons as soon as possible.

"I'll let you know about your lessons once I get them set up." Ms. Grissom walked around the room tapping the screens. "I think it's about time for you to get to lunch, then on to your afternoon classes. If anyone asks, you can tell them you're a level five feeler."

Skylar got out of the chair and headed for the door. "I guess that's something." It was a lot more than his mother would've been comfortable with. He just hoped Del wasn't going to be upset about him ranking higher than Del did.

9
Staying In School

AS THE school week progressed, Skylar fell into the pattern of his roommates and classmates. The space station had panels that opened and closed at set times during the day to simulate a Sol Three twenty-four standard hour pattern of day and night most humans found comfortable. Since the days on Hummassa had been twenty-six standard hours, it took Skylar a few days to get used to the shorter routine. He felt like time was flying past, and the end of the school week showed up too quickly.

"So, what do we do on the weekends?" Skylar asked as he settled into his chair at the lunch table next to Del and across from Solaria. It hadn't taken them long to develop a pattern of eating together. Although she had other friends in school, just like Del did, Solaria had latched onto the two of them for reasons she never explained, and Skylar didn't want to pry. Even if she was a bit moody at times, she was fun to be around and people tended not to piss her off.

"That depends," Solaria replied as she cut a piece of belesk, a small antelope native to Pantheria. Like a lot of her food, she ate it raw, something Skylar was slowly becoming accustomed to.

Skylar waited for her to continue, but she popped the meat in her mouth and chewed thoughtfully. "On what?" he finally asked after she swallowed.

"On what you want to do and what kind of credits you have. They normally have a shuttle that goes to

Aranack, the one human-habitable planet in the system, or sometimes they send the school ship to the Galaxeria if there are enough of us who have signed up to go." She frowned as she cut her next piece. "I'm not sure they'd let you go yet."

He set down his fork and stared at her. "What is the Galaxeria, and why wouldn't they let me go?"

Del came to his rescue as Solaria started chewing her next bite. "The Galaxeria is a massive shopping center that takes up one of the largest space stations in the galaxy. They have everything you could ever want for sale there. I've only been twice. It's a huge adventure and we should definitely try to go sometime, although it can also be extremely overwhelming. And they probably won't let you go yet because you haven't mastered your psi shielding yet. If you go out without mastering shielding, there's too much of a chance that you might pick something up that can upset you, or you could start broadcasting your emotions and influence the people around you." He shook his head. "You're a little behind the rest of us. They wouldn't want an untrained feeler loose in the galaxy."

It was Skylar's turn to frown. Ever since they'd tested him for psi skills and he came back high in feeler, they'd put him in special training classes. So far, he hadn't proven overly adept at any of the classes, particularly the shielding class. Shielding was supposed to keep a psi from picking up too much and from broadcasting too much.

"So, I've got to wait until I'm good at shielding before I can even think of leaving the academy?" The idea made him feel trapped. He wanted to master every skill so he could go do things the normal kids did without worrying about stuff like being overwhelmed by strong emotions.

Solaria shrugged. "Either that or wear a dampening bracelet. That'll mute your powers to the point you'll be all but useless. Unless you get upset and short it out." She smiled and looked at Del. "Remember that one field trip when the Volarian kid shorted out his bracelet and gave everyone in the spaceport his fear of spiders? That family of arachnoids was so terrified of each other that they had to undergo therapy before they could get in their ship and leave the port." She rolled her eyes and giggled. "That was priceless."

"And," Del sighed, "that's why they don't like to let the untrained psychics off the station without being sure nothing will happen. As I recall, it took over a week of therapy with a level eight reader to get them over it, and the academy had to foot the bill. Old Fussy Pants was mad for weeks."

"Old Fussy Pants?" Skylar asked as he set his fork on his now-empty plate.

"Oh yeah, you haven't met the principal, Mr. Fuspatula, yet," Del said. "When you meet him, you'll understand why we all call him Old Fussy Pants. It's part irony and part funny."

Skylar knew how kids tended to give teachers and school administrators strange and often rude nicknames. "Okay, now you've got me both intrigued and repelled."

Before they could continue, Ms. Grissom appeared at their table. "Skylar, can I interrupt your lunch? I need to talk to you."

Something in the counselor's tone caused Skylar's heart to skip. He nodded. "Sure." Standing, he glanced at his friends. "Catch you guys next class." He hoped it wasn't anything major. Maybe it was good news, like they had found a long-lost family member who had lots of money and was prepared to take care of Skylar... but for the first time since he arrived on the station, he thought about leaving his new friends and didn't like the idea. He liked Del and Solaria and wanted to keep them around.

Solaria gestured farewell with her fork as she chewed another bite of meat.

"Sure," Del said. "I'll even throw your garbage in the recycler."

"Thanks." It made Skylar feel good having friends willing to clean up after him when something unexpected came up.

Trailing Ms. Grissom, Skylar tried, unsuccessfully, to push back the fear of uncertainty that rose up in him. There were too many possibilities for what she might want. He had no idea about that might influence how things were going to go.

"It's good that you're making friends," Ms. Grissom said as they cleared the big double doors of the cafeteria. "And Del Aduncus and Solaria Uncia are excellent students. Although I didn't realize they were friends."

"I don't think they really were before I came this week," Skylar said. "But they're both really nice. Well, Solaria is a bit moody." He reminded himself that psychics really appreciated everyone being honest and could tell when people weren't being so.

Ms. Grissom chuckled. "She's a Pantherian. They tend to be rather fluid in their emotions. But don't worry. Once one befriends you, you have a friend for life. They're extremely loyal."

"That's what Del said after he got over the initial fear of being her friend." Skylar had also been a bit afraid of her too, but the fact that her uncle Phil had been the one who found Skylar had opened the way to their friendship, and that made all three of them happy.

"Yes, the two of them as friends seems a bit odd, but I think you're a good influence on them." She held the door to her office for him. "I'm getting good reports from your teachers. They all find you very intelligent and quick on the uptake. There is concern that you seem to have some mental blocks about mastering your psi skills, and that might be why you're having trouble learning to shield. I figure this has to do with the fears your mother instilled in you, and you'll overcome them soon and blossom. Most of the psychic teachers claim you'll have great potential once you embrace your powers."

She walked around behind her desk and Skylar sat in the chair he'd occupied his first day.

He wiped his sweaty hands on his pants as the feeling of unease grew. "Is that why you asked me in here?"

Ms. Grissom shook her head. "No. It appears that you'll be staying with us here at Stars' End Academy. And 'how' is a bit of a mystery."

Skylar straightened in his chair, his heart pounding furiously. "You've found my family?" If his mother never mentioned them, but the academy found them in just over a week, he wondered why his mother had been hiding from them and not the other way around. The more he thought about that, the more he thought it might have been her running from his father's psychic abilities.

"We're not sure." Her fingers danced across her desktop computer pad. The shimmer of a holographic projection formed over the center of the desk. The projection showed what appeared to be a bank transfer notice. "This morning, we received a deposit in your name. It's large enough to cover your next three years here at Stars' End."

Large enough to cover his next three years? Who would do that for him? Was his family rich or something? Skylar gulped and he rubbed his hands on his pants again. "Three years? Who sent it?"

"That's where the mystery is." Ms. Grissom's fingers continued to dance across her desk. "The deposit was made via a credit transfer from the Central Galaxy

Bank. Mr. Fuspatula has been in conference with his contact at the bank and was assured that the account it came from is a legitimate account and that all the codes for the transfer were correct. But it can't be traced beyond that."

Skylar slumped in his chair as the implications of the announcement registered. "So, we don't know who sent the money?" His future was safe for the next three years, but his past was still obscure. For a moment, he thought he might get some answers.

She frowned, and a wave of soothing energy flowed from her to him. "Yes and no. We received a coded transmission about the same time as the money was sent. I asked our IT guy to try to trace it back to him, but so far, he hasn't had any luck."

"Him?" Skylar sat up straighter again. Could this be a grandfather or uncle?

"Yes. Based on the message, we're assuming it's from a man." Ms. Grissom nodded. "Here's the message that was sent. It was text only, but I had it synthesized for you. The principal and I both felt it would be better if someone was with you when you got the message. I've had the original text forwarded to your account so you'll have a permanent copy." She tapped on her desk and a message began to play.

"Hello, Skylar," said a clear electronic voice. "I didn't know of your existence until a few days ago, when your DNA profile came across my desk. I've had the DNA cross-referenced to my own and your mother's. It is conclusive that you are my son."

The blood drained from Skylar's face. Son? His father was still alive? Why had his mother lied to him about the man dying in a shuttle accident?

The electronic voice continued. "I'm sorry that your mother is gone. I believed that she died in a shuttle accident nearly sixteen years ago. That's why I never looked for her or you. Even though I cannot openly acknowledge you, I'll do what I can to make sure you have a good basis for life from this point on. The Stars' End Academy is a very fine establishment and known for helping some of the galaxy's best psychics reach their full potential. You'll be in good hands there. Have a good life." The message ended.

Skylar sat numbly staring at Ms. Grissom's desk without really seeing the counselor as she got up and came around to him. So, his father was still alive, but wouldn't acknowledge him. What did he mean by that? What was Skylar supposed to do now? His father wanted him to have a good life, but he was all alone.

Ms. Grissom touched his shoulder. "It's a hard message. I understand that."

Skylar looked at her. For a moment, her calming aura pushed at him, but he rode his anger and pushed back against her efforts at manipulation. "Don't try to control me!"

She yanked back her hand with a shocked look.

"How can you understand? I bet both of your parents are still alive and love you. My mother is *dead!* My father wants to pay me off and leave me out here on the edge of space so I don't get in the way of his life! There's no way you can understand what I'm going through. I'm all alone! He made it perfectly clear that I'm going to stay that way until I make my own way in life and can find a family of my own!"

He stood and ran from the room. He ignored the stares and complaints from his fellow students and the academy staff as he ran from the office in no discernible direction. Around him, people began shouting. It seemed like their voices were everywhere. There wasn't anywhere he could go to get away from the sound.

He clamped his hands over his ears, hoping to block out some of the background noise, but it continued just as loud as it had been before he covered his ears. Skylar lost all sense of direction as he sought a place of quiet, where he could escape from the clamor. There was just so much *shouting*. He had to get away, and he ran until he couldn't run anymore.

10
Here There Are Cows

"WHY IS he here?" asked a quiet, mellow voice.

"I don't know," an equally peaceful voice replied. *"Maybe he came to feed us. But feeding time isn't for a little while yet, and he doesn't have any food."*

Skylar's head pounded. People still shouted in the distance. He didn't want to open his eyes, and kept his hands clamped over his ears. In the back of his mind, he knew that eventually, the shouting would go away, but the cacophony overpowered him. It was like the entire academy had picked that moment to scream at him. It hurt, and he wanted it to stop.

"Skylar." A soft voice intruded on the overwhelming noise, almost like the tweeting of a bird trying to compete with the sound of a celestial rock band set on overload. The softness startled him. He struggled to focus on the voice.

"Who are you?" The training he'd been undergoing came back, and it felt right to answer with a thought. He might not have much luck shielding, but sending wasn't a problem.

"I'm a friend. Skylar, just relax." The voice carried a soothing feeling. It reminded him of the gentle rhythm of the ocean he and his mother had visited on Hummassa the previous summer.

"I'll try. Will it make everyone stop shouting?" He took a deep breath, trying to relax the way his psi-trainers had been showing him. It still felt clumsy and strange to do it that way. Nothing made sense.

"Pay attention to my voice. Focus on me. It will help block everyone else out." The voice grew more prominent amidst the background noise.

"Keep talking to me," Skylar said. *"It's helping. Everyone else is getting quieter."* For a moment, as his concentration on the voice wavered and his hope jumped, the shouting tried to reassert itself. He panicked. The gentle rhythm of his breathing faltered. He struggled to find the voice again.

"Deep breaths, Skylar. Just focus on me. Don't let anything disrupt your focus on me."

Skylar took another deep breath. *"Okay, so what do I do to keep focusing on you?"*

"We'll just keep talking, how's that? And as we talk, tell me about what you like here at Stars' End. There've got to be things you like."

"I'm making friends. They're nice. Del and Solaria are really cool, even if Del is a bit of a brain, and Solaria can be moody."

The voice chuckled. *"Yes, that is true on both counts. It's good that you're finding friends here. That's not always easy in a new place. So, what else do you like? What about the farm? A lot of the kids from less-developed worlds like the farm. I think it reminds them of home."*

Skylar took another deep breath and was surprised that the musky, sweet smell of the cow barn filled his nose. *"Yeah, I like the farm. The animals are cool. I've always liked animals."* The shouting receded further, as if the angry mob was moving away from him.

"Good, focus on that. Focus on the animals."

"Do you think he might feed us soon?" the soft pleasant voice asked, counter to what the other voice was saying. *"It really is rude to come visit us and not bring us food."*

Skylar slowly opened his eyes and pulled his hands away from his ears. He looked up into the face of an elder Tursiops. Behind the gray face and white hair stood Ms. Grissom, Del, and Solaria. Beyond them, a couple of cows looked over their short stall walls.

The elder Tursiops smiled. "It seems that you've come back to us, young Mr. Mars."

"What happened?" Skylar tried to remember how he got from the counselor's office to the cow barn. It was just a haze, running through the station trying to get away from the voices.

"What do you remember?" the Tursiops asked.

Skylar looked up at Ms. Grissom. His throat tightened with regret. He felt like he'd disappointed her in some way. He'd never gotten so angry at an adult before. "I was shouting at Ms. Grissom after she played the message from my father. Then everyone started shouting back at me." He shook his head. "It was like the whole school was yelling and screaming at me."

The Tursiops nodded, then frowned. "I think you may be stronger than any of us realized. I don't normally ask this of new psychics, but I'd like to put a dampening bracelet on you for a while."

"A dampening bracelet?" Skylar remembered Solaria or Del saying something about them recently, but couldn't remember what. It was still hard to put thoughts together. He was tired and hoped things would clear after a few minutes.

"Yes. Until you get control of your abilities, you're going to be a danger to yourself and anyone around you of lower level."

"Which apparently is a good portion of the school," Solaria muttered just loud enough for him to hear.

The man looked over his shoulder at her. "While I appreciate your assistance in finding young Mr. Mars, your presence may no longer be needed, Ms. Uncia, if you cannot hold your tongue."

"She'll be quiet, Grandfather," Del said, then looked at Solaria. "Won't you?"

She bowed her head as Skylar realized who he was talking to—Del's grandfather. Then Professor Aduncus turned back to him. "I don't want you to have to wear the bracelet very long. At this point in your training, it could be detrimental to your development. I just want to be sure that you master shielding both your thoughts and emotions from others. You have to find your center. If you can't do that, you'll lose control every time your emotions run rampant."

Skylar shook his head, trying to understand what Del's grandfather was saying. "But I thought I was just able to pick up emotions. Emotions shouldn't sound like people shouting at me, should they?"

"Skylar, my boy, you're far more than a feeler, although a feeler you are. You're also a reader, and from the explosive way your reader powers have come to light, I'm going to say that you're a fairly powerful one too. If you thought that the whole academy was shouting at you, that means you were tapping into the minds of a large portion of the station." He paused and sighed. "That would be a major feat for me, and I'm a level ten reader. You also shared your fears with those around you. Luckily, your projection skills are going to take some strengthening, or we might have had a good portion of the school incapacitated. Can you understand why I think we need to put a dampening bracelet on you for a while?"

"I think so." Skylar nodded. "But how long will I have to wear it?" He was becoming a danger, just like his mother had said all psychics were. But he didn't want to be a danger—he wanted to learn to control his skills.

Professor Aduncus shrugged. "That's entirely up to you. If you can master your abilities, you won't have to wear it long. I understand that you're already in class to learn shielding." He stood up from the straw-covered floor and stretched. "I think it would be best if, for the time being, I took over your training. I am the head of the reader's department and the strongest reader in this part of space." He looked at Skylar as he offered him a hand up. *"Or so I thought."*

"That's a very good idea," Ms. Grissom said, sounding relieved.

Skylar dusted the dirt and hay off his gray synth pants. "Ms. Grissom, I want to say that I'm sorry for what happened. I didn't mean to get so upset." His stomach knotted as he got the words out. He didn't like having to apologize for his actions, and losing control like he'd just done made it worse.

She smiled. "Remember that in the future. You can't let your emotions get the better of you. But that's okay. You've been through a lot, more than most of us ever go through in a whole life. I accept your apology."

"Thank you." He nodded.

"Now, Mr. Mars, before you go wandering off, let's put this on you." Professor Aduncus held up a small black band. It looked a bit like a leather bracelet.

"Does it matter which arm?" Skylar asked, trying to decide which one it would look better on. He hoped he'd be able to pull the sleeve of his shirt over it, since he didn't doubt that everyone on the station knew what the band was. He didn't want to give them more reasons to look down on him beyond the fact that he was still the new kid.

Professor Aduncus shook his head. "Whichever you prefer. Remember, it will come off when we're training."

Skylar held out his right arm. "Will I be able to take it off if I want?"

"Yes. Well, you'll need help, but it won't be locked on if that's what has you worried. Due to safety protocols, it takes two hands." Professor Aduncus closed the band over Skylar's wrist. "So, you'll need someone to help you get it off and on."

The effect was almost instantaneous: a strange quiet settled over him. His mind was almost crystal clear. Skylar stood perfectly still for a moment. He looked past his friends, teacher, and counselor at the cows. The two bovines stared at him with big brown eyes. He almost expected them to ask about dinner, but they were silent.

"Are you okay, Skylar?" Del asked.

"Yeah. It's just so quiet. I never realized things could be so quiet." Skylar looked at the bracelet. Upon closer inspection, there was a series of fine wires and circuits running through the leather-like material. He ran his fingers over it. It felt like the native clothes Teir and the other Hummassans used to wear, but had enough of a plastic feel that he knew it wasn't.

"You've been picking up on more than you realized for a while," said the professor. "It's not uncommon for budding psychics to perceive background emotions and thoughts for years before their powers actively manifest. I'd say you found your way to Stars' End just in time. I'm amazed this talent didn't show up in your testing. Now, why don't you three take the rest of the afternoon off? We're in the farm area, so go find a tree to relax under, or run off some energy. I'll let your teachers know you'll be missing the rest of your classes for the day. Mr. Mars, I know tomorrow is a rest day, but we need to get that bracelet off you as quickly as possible. You'll report to my office after breakfast. If you don't know where it is, Mr. Aduncus can show you."

Skylar nodded. "Yes, sir."

Professor Aduncus smiled. "Good, now off with all of you. Relax and have some fun."

11
Field Trip

"COME ON, Skylar!" Del pounded on the bathroom door. "If you make us late, I'm going to be really angry."

"Just a minute." Skylar ran a brush through his brown hair and finally nodded at his reflection in the mirror. It was his first field trip and chance to get off the station. He wanted to look decent.

He opened the door and Del nearly ran him over to get into the bathroom. "I thought you didn't take a shower in the morning?" Skylar shouted at the already-closed door. There was so much about the other species he shared Stars' End with that he was still learning. Sometimes he felt like he was never going to learn the ins and outs of living out here.

"This isn't about the shower," Del shouted back.

Skylar turned to Fin, who was busy tucking in the coverlet on his bunk. "Okay, so what's his deal? This is just a field trip to some museum, right? Why's he getting so excited?"

Fin turned and looked at Skylar. "You have to understand Del. This is a chance to discover stuff he might not learn here at the academy. He wants to look his best in hopes of making an impression on someone at the museum who might be able to help him get a position when we graduate."

"What?" Skylar frowned, trying to understand. They still had a few years before they graduated. It didn't make any sense. "He's only fifteen. Why is he already thinking about making contacts for a future job?"

"He's a low-level feeler. Most of the Tursiops who don't find jobs as psychics end up going into aquaculture back on Tursipia. It's what our race evolved for. Del's too smart for that, so he's already on the lookout for opportunity he can use his brains to get ahead. A museum would be a perfect place for him. It's filled with knowledge, and there would always be something new to learn."

Skylar pursed his lips and thought about it. "Okay, that makes sense. He's probably thinking first impressions and stuff like that." The only first impression Skylar really thought about making was with the Boarisk raiders when he caught up to them and instilled fear in their entire race. He hadn't made much progress on things, other than starting a diary of where they struck and what kind of methods they used in their attacks on various planets. The problem he kept running into was there didn't seem to be a pattern he could detect.

Fin nodded. "Exactly."

Connor burst into the room. "Are you guys ready yet or not? The line's already forming at the airlock."

"We're just waiting for Del," Fin replied. He picked up his small pack from his bunk. "We're all packed and ready to go."

"Me too." Skylar shouldered his own pack. They'd all been told to carry a day and a half's worth of clothes and necessities to cover them through the trip. It wasn't much, but it would be enough for them to get by. Apparently, everything else they were going to need would be provided at the museum.

"Mars." Connor frowned. "I still don't understand why they're letting you go. After your outburst last week, the last thing we need is you losing it in a public place."

Skylar held up his right arm with the dampening bracelet on easy display. The only time it had been off his skin in a week had been during his training sessions with

Professor Aduncus, which were coming along agonizingly slowly. He really hoped he'd get the hang of psi skills quickly, but even the little stuff seemed beyond him. "I don't think I'm a danger to anyone right now."

Connor's frown deepened, then he smiled. "Unless they get a good look at your face." He snatched his bag off his bunk and ran for the hall.

"Yeah, well, your face is worse!" Skylar shouted after him.

Del emerged from the bathroom with his bluish hair perfectly groomed. "What is with you humans and having to comment on each other's faces?"

Skylar shrugged. "Hey, I didn't start it. It wasn't something that we did on Hummassa. Connor started the whole thing a few days ago." It didn't make much sense and Skylar had wondered, but not bothered to ask, if the comments on how bad someone's face looked was some kind of hazing ritual.

Fin sighed as Del grabbed his pack and the three walked toward the hall. "Yeah, we all know when it started. It's getting old already. We may have to put an end to it before it gets out of hand."

"That would be nice." As he agreed, Skylar silently wondered how Fin and Del, since Fin said "we" would put an end to Connor's face comments. He was ready for Connor to move on to something that at least sounded a bit more mature.

Just like Connor said, there was a line forming in the entrance hall. There were already several people behind Connor as Skylar, Del, and Fin joined them.

The broad shoulders and torso with long gray-dabbled white hair cascading down in front of him looked familiar. Skylar touched the shoulder. "Hey, Solaria."

The Pantherian spun around with a growl. The eyes looking at him were a deep brown, not his friend's crystal blue. "I am not who you think, *human*." The last word came out as a snarl.

Not expecting the harsh reply from an unfriendly face, Skylar stumbled backward a pace. "Sorry. I thought you were Solaria."

"Oh, did you?" The Pantherian's frown deepened. "Do I look remotely female to you? Or are you one of those humans who think that all the other species look the same, regardless of sex?"

"Hey, it was an honest mistake." Skylar squared his shoulders and stared up into the guy's eyes. He knew the guy could shred him without much trouble, but he didn't like getting pushed around for a something he didn't exactly understand. With a lot of species, it was hard to tell one sex from the other when faced with a person's back. His hair did look a lot like Solaria's, and he had the same build. From behind, they could've been twins.

"Oh, will you stop posturing, Mutanio?" Solaria said from behind Skylar. "So, he still gets confused. That's no reason to go after Skylar. He's a nice guy." She moved so she stood between them. "Now back down, before I have to put you on the floor." She growled slightly. "You don't want me to do that in front of nearly a quarter of the school, do you?"

Mutanio fell two steps back from her. "I'm not afraid of you, Solaria. I didn't know you had a thing for humans."

She sighed and flexed her claws. "You know, you're really starting to tick me off. Oh, and most of the people around here saw you back up from me just now. Do you think they don't realize that means you're at least a little bit afraid of me?"

"Alright, we're going to begin boarding now!" Mr. Corda's voice rang out, amplified by the school's public address system. "Please behave yourselves. We cannot have any incidents this time."

Solaria cast a last glare at Mutanio. "Leave my friends alone or we *will* have trouble." She turned her back on him and looked at Skylar. "So, you ready for your first field trip? These things are always a lot of fun."

"Nearly a day and a half in close quarters with the likes of Connor and Mutanio?" Skylar sighed. "Yeah, it's going to be a lot of fun." He hoped nothing would go wrong, but with so many kids along, it was a distinct possibility. At least he had Solaria and Del with him. Having friends helped him feel more confident in everything. He just hoped wherever he was, Teir was okay. He missed Teir almost as much as he missed his mother, and there was still no word from Hummassa about him.

"I WANT you to take a deep breath and relax," Del told Skylar.

Skylar frowned. "If I still have the dampening bracelet on, how will this help? It's not like I can use my powers now, even if I wanted to." Not that he could do much with them if he tried. Everything else in school had come easily; even if he wasn't great at any one thing, the building blocks seemed simple.

Del shook his head. "I still think you'd be so much better off if you'd actually been trained several years ago in the basics. Using your psi powers is like using your body. It's a matter of getting used to doing things. I really doubt you crawled out of your mother, stood up and walked out of the hospital room."

"Look at that funky ear of his. You never know, he might've walked seconds after birth." Pathal Santos plopped down at the workstation next to Skylar.

Solaria glared at him. "Well, if he did, he's definitely far more evolved than you'll ever be. Don't you and your groupies have some silly little star-counting game to keep your tiny minds occupied? Or maybe you need to go play with the nav computer so we go sailing through the wrong stargate and into a black hole."

Pathal grimaced at her. "You know, I think I saw a rat in the rear of the ship. Maybe you need to go chase it. That *is* why they let your kind into school, isn't it? To keep the rodents under control?"

Solaria's smile showed all her fangs. "Then why are there so many of you corp-brats around if we're trying to get rid of the rodents?"

"Students!" Professor Corda's voice blared over the ship's intercom system. "We're approaching the stargate. For those of you who like the view, I suggest getting near a window within the next two minutes."

"Cool." Ignoring Pathal's presence, Skylar turned to look out the window as the ship approached the huge portal hanging in space just outside the star's gravity well. The show was similar to the first one he'd seen going through the stargate with Phil, but Skylar stayed glued to the window until all the excitement was over and they had entered normal space again at their destination solar system. He didn't think he'd ever get tired of going through stargates, or space travel in general. He understood the principles of it, and it was simple math and physics, but the wonder of it caught hold of him and held him tight.

When he looked away from the window, Pathal had left their table. "I guess he got bored?"

Solaria shrugged. "You know how most of these limited-intelligence types are. If you're not paying attention to them, they wander off. Why do you find the stargates so interesting?"

"They're cool." Skylar didn't attempt to hide his excitement. "If I thought I could get away with it, I'd be up in the flight deck with the pilot. Space flight is awesome. I'd love to get my own ship like Phil and spend time flying around the universe."

"If you're really as strong as some of the murmurings I'm catching from my grandfather, it's possible," Del said. "He's really expecting you to grow in your abilities. The more powerful a psi is, the more in demand they are. The rest of us have to get by on our brains or who we know."

Skylar cocked an eyebrow at his friend. "And psychics aren't getting by on their brains?"

Solaria chuckled.

"That's not what I meant and you know it," Del mumbled. "Eventually your brain is just going to be another muscle for you, which brings us back to your focus exercises. You've got to get your brain used to getting quiet and centered. Just because you have the dampening bracelet on doesn't mean you can't work on quieting your mind. You might be surprised how relaxing and peaceful it feels."

"We've got another few hours before we get to the museum," Solaria said. "You might as well get some practice. I bet his grandfather put him up to this to keep you moving along. The sooner you're under control, the sooner the Professor gets to work with someone else and you get your free time back. Unless you're like Del and don't like free time."

"I like free time just fine," Del sniped. "It's just more interesting when it's spent in a library or a museum. We can never get enough new knowledge."

"My point exactly." Solaria yawned and stretched. "Tell you what. You two sit here and work on Skylar's mind muscles, and I'm going to go ruffle Mutanio's fur a bit. He's always good for a laugh, particularly since he knows I *can* wipe the floor with him." She stood and strolled toward the back of the ship where her fellow Pantherian had disappeared shortly after they came on board.

Skylar waited until her broad shoulders disappeared through the doorway before turning to Del. "Can she really do that? I know she's big and strong, but he's a guy of the same species."

Del chuckled and leaned back in his chair. "Yeah, she can. In fact, there was an incident last year, when she was a little"—he made a tiny motion with his thumb and forefinger—"smaller than she is now. I don't know all the details, but they both ended up in Ms. Grissom's office for anger counseling. Several of the holo-portraits in the entry hall had to be replaced, and after their meeting with Ms. Grissom, Mutanio spent a couple of hours in the med bay."

Skylar's eyes widened. "She put him in med bay?"

"Yeah." Del nodded, then leaned forward and put his elbows on the table. "Like I said, I don't know much, but he normally gives her a wide berth around school. I've heard that female Pantherians are a lot more dangerous than males and I can believe it. I'm actually glad she's on our side. Most of the girls tend to avoid her too. I think she scares them. She might just be lonely, and it's safe for her to hang around us."

"I really don't care why she's hanging around. She's nice and it's good to have her with us from time to time." When Del's face darkened for a moment, Skylar hastily added. "Hey, don't worry. You were my first friend here and you're my best friend." As he said it, he remembered Teir back on Hummassa. Teir had been his best friend for years. But he was slowly coming to terms with his past being gone. All he had was his present and his future.

12
Walking With The Past

SINCE THE school ship they rode in wasn't atmosphere worthy, it took two tightly loaded shuttle trips to move all the students from the ship to the museum entrance. A series of Romanesque columns formed the front of the massive building that looked like it might actually be larger than Stars' End Academy.

Skylar watched the whole thing come into view as the second shuttle descended. The planet housing the museum appeared well developed. Much of the continent they headed toward was occupied by huge buildings that had very little to differentiate them. There wasn't much in the way of green that could be spotted out of the shuttle window. It was mostly white, gray, black, and silver. Skylar shuddered slightly, remembering the jungle of Hummassa where he used to hike, explore, and play. He missed the massive trees and the peace and quiet they brought. This planet didn't appear to have any of that.

He turned to Del for a moment. "What planet did you say this was?"

Del sighed. "The Museum of Space and Time is located on the planet Nesbit. We're closer to the center of the Galactic Council than I've ever been before. All of the worlds around here have been colonized for at least a thousand years. The amount of knowledge they all possess is staggering. There's little in the way of science or art that hasn't found its way here at one time or another. People can go an entire lifetime and not experience everything that's here."

"Even if their lack of open spaces is somewhat disturbing," Solaria added with a visible quiver. "I still don't get why so many races think a planet is civilized only if they conquer all the wild out of it. One of these days we'll get you to Pantheria, and you'll understand how a civilized race can still manage to embrace a wild world."

Skylar smiled and turned back to the window as the shuttle came in for its landing. The planet was so sterile there wasn't even any dust kicked up as the thrusters fired and the ship settled on the shining steel landing pad. "I'd like to see that. Hummassa still had a lot of wild left to it. It was nice. But this is good too, just a different kind of good."

A couple minutes later, they stood on the vast marble steps that led up to the huge doors—large enough that any of the races belonging to the Galactic Council could enter easily. A teacher Skylar didn't know instructed them to follow her into the building. As they entered the hall, Professor Corda's droning voice drifted back to them in the wake of the group from the first shuttle making their way out of the entrance hall.

The Professor's stand-in, Mrs. Tyler, was a human and proceeded to give them the overview of the official tour, which would take them nearly twelve hours to complete. There would be a couple of rests, along the way with a meal in the middle of the tour.

"Twelve hours in a museum?" Skylar asked. Suddenly the excitement of the outing turned to a fear of utter boredom. He hoped there were going to be a lot of interactive displays.

"The biggest, most intense museum in the entire galaxy!" Del grinned. "And that's only the stuff on display. I wish we could get a behind-the-scenes tour, but I heard those cost thousands of credits and are planned years in advance. It's enough that they had to clear out the museum for us."

Skylar looked at his friend in disbelief. "What? They cleared out the place for us? Why?"

"When the Stars' End Academy wants to bring their students on a field trip, most places set it up so we get the best private tours available," Del explained. "Most of our parents pay big credits for us to attend, even if it is on a sliding scale based on our psi talent levels. I hear some of the corp-brats who don't have any powers pay a lot more, but they think the education is worth it."

"Or, you could just say they're afraid of us." Solaria graced them with her toothiest smile. "After all, who really wants a group of partially-trained psychics mixed with a bunch of rich corp-brats running loose with the general populace? It might not end well. But at least this way, we don't have a bunch of people staring at us while we stare at the stuff in here." She looked up at one of the huge statues in the first gallery. "You know, Skylar, this guy kinda looks like you."

Del shook his head and put his hands on his hips as he stared up at the thirty-foot-tall statue. "I don't know. I mean, that's Caffar O'Byrne, founder of O'Byrne Corporation. He's one of the main people responsible for humans expanding out through the galaxy. Or are you trying to say that because he's human, he looks like Skylar?"

Solaria turned and glared at Del. "You should know I'm not a species-ist. I would never say that just because they're both humans, they look alike. How insensitive do you think I am?"

Del's gray skin paled to almost white. "I'm sorry. So why do you think they look alike?"

"Yeah. I mean, he's got a beard and long hair." Skylar stared up at the statue, then backed up a few steps to get a better view. He didn't see a resemblance.

Solaria started her explanation with a bit of hand waving and gesturing. "Now, you've got to remember that I'm a predator by nature. As a predator, I naturally observe everything and everyone around me for weakness. You didn't realize I did that, did you?"

They both shook their heads. Skylar had never stopped to think that Solaria was always commenting on the least little thing that was out of place due to her being a predator, looking for flaws that could be detrimental to those around her. He wondered if she was always just waiting for an excuse to pounce on someone.

"Well, I do," she continued. "So, since I know what Skylar looks like, right down to his scarred ear, when I saw this statue I immediately noticed the similarities in nose, eyes, and mouth."

Skylar studied the statue's face and tried to compare it to how his own face looked in the mirror. He shook his head. "I don't know." He wondered if she was saying something about him starting to look more mature.

The teacher called for the group to follow her out of the gallery. Skylar paused for a parting glance at Caffar O'Byrne. He stood as one of the greats in the creation of the Galactic Council. He was right there with the Floxian who had built the first pair of stargates, making it easier to move across the galaxy. Both families were among the richest in the universe. It was rumored that the O'Byrne family actually owned their own solar system.

"Come on Skylar," Del urged. "We don't want to miss anything important."

Skylar realized all the other students had disappeared and Del and Solaria stood in the entrance to the next galley waiting for him. "Okay, I'm coming. I still don't see the resemblance." He felt stupid for staring at the statue and making his friends fall behind the group. Quickening his step, he rushed so they could catch up with everyone else.

Solaria laughed. "Maybe you will when you get old enough to grow a beard."

Skylar couldn't help but mirror her laugh. "Maybe. I just hope I can see the universe the same way he saw the galaxy. That would be awesome." As they followed their group, Skylar thought back to what Phil said about getting to explore, and the vast amount of the universe that was still out there waiting to be properly discovered. Entire star clusters and systems bore the names of the brave men and women who'd discovered them. Would there one day be a Skylar Mars system or star? He thought that would be awesome.

13
Solaria Gets Protective

AFTER TWELVE hours in the museum, Skylar wasn't the only student to fall asleep fairly quickly after they returned to the school ship and got into their seats. The joy of exploring the undiscovered universe filled his dreams. There were stars and planets out there that no one had ever heard of, comets that had only shown up as fuzzy streaks on distant telescopic images, and he was finding them all. He had a ship that looked a lot like Phil's, but Del, Solaria, and Teir were there with him. Every time they touched down on a new world, there was a new adventure. There was a tropical world with another planet so close it was like they were touching.

The inhuman screaming started for the first time since he put on the dampening bracelet.

"Give me that!" Solaria shouted, shattering Skylar's sleep, ripping him from his dream. He opened his eyes as Solaria jerked something round out of Pathal's hands.

"Give that back, we found it and it's ours!" the dark haired corp-brat replied.

"Not anymore." Solaria turned and protectively cradled the thing in her arm. "Can't you feel it's alive? You're scaring it." She glared at Pathal and two of his cronies. "Now, I don't care where you found it. I'm not letting you scare this poor little one, whatever it is." She dropped her voice and flashed a claw with the hand that wasn't cradling the thing. "Back down human, or find out why my planet was quarantined for three hundred years."

Pathal gulped and retreated to his seat, muttering about how the pig at the museum wasn't supposed to be there and the egg was theirs by right. But he didn't try and force Solaria to give it back to him. He was dumb, but he wasn't *that* stupid.

Solaria ran a hand over the object in the crook of her arm and walked back to the seat next to Skylar, where she'd been when he'd dropped off to sleep.

All thoughts of sleep were gone as he peered at her to see what she'd rescued from the bully. "What is it?" Skylar kept his voice low.

"An egg of some kind." Solaria continued to stroke it and started to purr softly. It was something he'd never heard her do.

"So, you're feeling a life inside it?" Del rubbed at his eyes. "You know, you're lucky that you and Pathal didn't wake the whole ship, shouting like that."

She pursed her lips and continued to purr. "I wasn't going to let him torture this poor little life like that, tossing it around like a ball. I could feel its distress, even in the egg. It has to be close to hatching. Every life deserves a chance, particularly one that hasn't even seen the light of day yet."

Skylar stared at the egg. It was about twice the size of his fist, bright orange with a few red splotches on it. "Any idea what kind of egg it is?"

Solaria shook her head. "No, but it is kinda pretty."

Del pulled out his school tablet. "Luckily, we've got a connection on the ship. So let's see what I can find." He danced his webbed fingers across the screen. "Based on color, there are over four thousand species, either avian or reptilian, in the known universe that could've laid it. Using the size as a criteria"—he frowned—"it would help if we had a scale and could weigh it."

"It weighs about 400 grams," Solaria said.

Skylar looked at her questioningly. He didn't understand how she could possibly know that.

She shrugged. "What? I'm a predator. Predators know these things."

"Details?" Skylar asked.

"Details."

Del sighed. "Even with that information, it only narrows it down to ten options." He frowned. "And unfortunately, the options can be kinda messy depending on what pops out of that thing."

"Like what?" Skylar glanced out the window. They were approaching the stargate. He wanted to watch the transition across the galaxy, but he doubted his friends would pause in their discussion to let him. He hoped they wouldn't see his distraction as being rude. He did want to know what Solaria had taken from Pathal, but he wanted to see their jaunt through the stargate more.

"Well." Del sighed again, this time a bit more dramatically. "Here are the options, in alphabetical order. An Anterian Alligator—they require three times their weight in raw meat within an hour of hatching or they die. The Carpathian Bat Bird is fairly helpless but has been known to bleed a handler dry if they aren't handled properly. They also have a nasty high-pitched scream. Now the Formisian Cow Bird is fairly harmless. All they do in the wild is push their siblings out of the nest so they can get all the food their parents bring in. With a…I can't pronounce this one." He flipped his tablet around so Skylar and Solaria could see a two-legged red lizard with large eyes and larger teeth. "That one also requires a lot of raw meat quickly."

Skylar turned to look at the picture, then looked back out the window as quickly as possible. He didn't bother saying that he really hoped that one was wrong. All the teeth bothered him.

"They look like they might be kinda fun to have around." Solaria looked down at the egg and continued to stroke it.

"The Marispian Cronozard interrupts the flow of time around it, but otherwise is fairly harmless. I really don't want it to be a Michellian Gluttenpeal. When they hatch, they consume everything they can get in their mouths until they burst. Once they burst, up to a dozen eggs are left behind." Del shuddered. "Yeah, don't want it to be one of those."

"Yeah, if it's one of those things, we're giving it back to Pathal and let it hatch in his dorm room." Skylar gave the idea a thumbs up. "That will take care of those pathetic corp-brats."

Solaria shook her head. "Nope, even a Michellian Gluttenpeal deserves better than to be tortured in its egg by those fools. Keep going, Del. I mean I guess we won't really know what it is until it hatches, but you're giving us some good info."

"The Rigelian Wren looks relatively harmless, although they do grow pretty large, largest songbird in the galaxy. Solar Drakes look interesting but there's not a lot of info on them. They seem fairly decent. Although it says they bond to telepaths." He looked from Skylar to Solaria. "You're both readers, so you might want to be careful around it. The Timathian Titmouse-"

Solaria's snicker cut him off. "I would love to know where the idea of a titmouse came from and why we seem to have them on every planet."

"Well, the first titmouse was named—" Del started to explain, but Skylar held up a hand.

"I think she was making a joke." He'd let his attention wander to Del's reading of the various things that might be in the egg. The light from outside the window alerted Skylar to the entrance of the stargate. Even not looking, Skylar still felt a little something as they entered the gate to be propelled across the galaxy and back to the system where Stars' End orbited. He tried to convince himself that it was just his imagination. No one could actually feel when a ship entered a stargate.

Del frowned at the two of them. "Fine, so on to the Unisconian Iguana. Again, relatively harmless, until it starts growing and doesn't stop until it's about the size of a small shuttle. And lastly, it could be a Zilobrathian Mini-Ostrich. Much like the standard Sol Three birds, but smaller."

"Smaller might not be such a bad thing, since we're in a school and all," Solaria purred.

Del frowned at her again as he laid his tablet on his workstation. "You do realize that you're probably not going to be able to keep whatever comes out of that thing? The faculty will have a fit that we're even bringing it back with us."

She clutched the egg to her chest. "*We're* not bringing the egg back. I am. If there's a problem with it when it hatches, if it's something I want to keep, I'll call my parents and they can come to school and get it for me or find some way of invoking the old rules about students being allowed a pet as long as they keep their grades up."

Skylar cocked his head and looked at the egg. "We're allowed pets?"

This gave Del the opportunity to explain how, since there are teachers with families in residence, that pets are allowed, but only under special conditions. Skylar had never had a pet. His mother said there were enough animals out in the woods around where they lived that he didn't need one in the house too. He wondered what it would be like to have a life that needed him to take care of it.

"OKAY, SO what are we going to do with it?" Del asked as they drew near Stars' End.

Skylar looked at him, trying to figure out what he was talking about. "Do with what?"

"The egg," Del gestured to the seat where Solaria was cradling it and still purring.

"We're keeping it," Solaria said. Her words were soft, and Skylar was thankful they were in a small cubby in the hallway. There weren't any other students around at the moment so no one could overhear their conversation.

Del rolled his eyes. "I can see that. But have you forgotten about the bioscanners as we exit the ship? They're going to detect something. We'll get stopped, and Ms. Grissom, Old Fussy Pants, or one of the teachers will come in and confiscate it."

It was something Skylar hadn't considered. When he'd gotten off Phil's ship and onto the school ship, nothing had made a sound, so he hadn't stopped to think about the scanners, which were most likely built into the walls of the airlock. That's where they always were in the games he played. "Do we have a way to shield it? Solaria, you've said you were good at shielding."

"We're both good at shielding," Del corrected him. "We'd be able to keep the teachers from sensing it once we get it on board, but the bioscanners are different from thoughts and emotions."

There was a slight bump that told Skylar they'd docked with Stars' End.

"Right, and remember to shield your mind about this little one from the teachers. Skylar's got his dampening bracelet, so we don't have to worry about his mind being read. We'll shield ourselves and the egg." Solaria slipped the egg into her shoulder bag and stood. "Now, just follow me. I've got an idea."

Skylar wanted to ask what her idea was, but there was a soft chime and the hall suddenly filled with the other students, all headed toward the airlock. He fell into step with Del who was trying to follow Solaria as she wove in and out of the rush of people like she wanted to be the first one off the ship. She slowed next to a boy about her height and matched his pace. Several other students made it through the airlock ahead of them, then the alarms went off.

Around Skylar and Del, several other students moaned and stopped moving forward. Over the heads of the people between them, Skylar saw Solaria wave to someone, and keep walking while the boy she'd been walking next to hollered, "It's just me."

Del chuckled.

Skylar glanced at him. "What's so funny?"

"That's Kaljin—he's a Kinajar. He's got a really fast metabolism and is always eating, particularly fruit and honeys. Every time he's on a field trip, the bioscanners stop him." Del grinned.

Suddenly Skylar understood. Solaria had walked into the airlock with someone she knew would trigger the sensor. If the teachers knew it too, they wouldn't think to stop her and see what she was carrying.

Ms. Grissom showed up and inspected the things Kaljin pulled out of his bag. They weren't close enough to hear what she had to say, but Kaljin's narrow shoulders slumped and he kept nodding. Ms. Grissom took the bag from him, then called out, "Sorry for the delay. If anyone else has something to declare, now is the time."

"I want to see it light up when you take the egg through," Pathal whispered in Skylar's ear. He'd gotten close enough while Skylar was paying attention to Ms. Grissom that Skylar jumped.

Del turned and glared as Skylar did. "What egg?" Del looked completely innocent.

Before Pathal could say anything more, the line surged forward and they were through the airlock without any other alarms.

IT DIDN'T take them long to find Solaria. She was in the common room near the cafeteria. Skylar didn't need to read her emotions to know something was wrong.

"Del, can you take my pack to the room? I'm going to go see what's wrong with Solaria."

Del took his pack. "Sure. I'd go with you, but I want to go send the museum curator a thank you for showing us around and giving us an awesome tour."

Skylar nodded. He'd watched Del spend the entire tour doing his best to impress the various museum employees they encountered, so he wasn't surprised at him wanting to do something polite. The odds were that, other than from the teachers, it was likely to be the only thank you the staff received. "Okay. You go do that. I'll catch up to you in a bit." He followed Solaria.

He found her sitting on one of the couches furthest from the door. She was just taking the egg out of her pack when he reached her. "Hey, is something wrong?"

Her furry face was set in a frown. It made her look angry and more than a little dangerous. "I've been thinking."

Skylar settled into the spot on the couch next to her pack. "About what?"

She started stroking the egg. "This little one. I don't think I can take it to my room. I don't think that my roommates will understand that I want to hatch it. Plus, our room is colder than galactic norm. That might not be good for the egg. None of the eggs this size come from cold climates."

That did sound like a major problem, and something Skylar hadn't considered. Without knowing what was inside the egg, they didn't know what kind of care it needed. "You're trying to decide what to do with it?"

Before she could answer, Pathal and his posse strolled past. The corp-brats all glared but didn't say anything to either of them.

Solaria warily watched them go by before she continued. "Yeah. I really want to keep it and help it hatch, but what if spending too much time in my room would kill it? What if my roommates kill it and eat it?"

"Eat it?" Skylar scrunched up his face. "What are your roommates?"

"Two of them are Pantherians like me, but the other one, Dorma—she's a Pinipedian. Some people think they are actually bigger predators than we are. She's a bit more aggressively predatory. I don't think her system would tolerate even slightly cooked meat, and she never eats vegetables. I think they put us all together as opposed to risking putting one of the more prey-based species with us." Solaria shook her head as she stroked the egg. "The egg just wouldn't be safe. Part of me says take it to a teacher and let them figure out what it is, and return it to where it belongs. I'd love to know how Pathal and his idiots got hold of it. Who was the pig they were talking about?"

"They might've stolen it from the museum, in which case we need to return it," Skylar suggested. Things housed in the museum belonged there, but he hadn't seen anything alive in there, and the egg was definitely alive.

"No. It was a museum, not a zoo. I didn't see or smell anything living there except us and the staff. I mean, they might've stolen it from someone, but it wasn't part of the museum proper." Her shoulders sagged. "I don't know what to do. I really want to see what it turns out to be. Watching those jerks abusing it triggered that protective mother instinct in me. My mom always said there was nothing more dangerous than a mother Pantherian. After what I felt as they tossed this egg around and feeling the little life inside knowing fear, I understood."

"If it can already feel fear, then it's fairly close to hatching."

Solaria nodded.

"We wouldn't need to keep it hidden very long, just long enough to see what it is, and then we can decide what to do with it. Would you be okay with me taking it? Our room is standard human temperature. Del and Fin wouldn't mind, and we can probably convince Connor to keep his mouth shut, at least until it hatches. Once it hatches, we'll work everything out, provided it's not a Michellian Gluttenpeal that eats all of us as soon as it hatches, its offspring consuming all the students and staff over the course of a few months until all that's left is Gluttenpeal eggs laying around waiting for some unsuspecting traveler to come by and take them to a planet where they can do it all over again."

"Putting it that way, I wonder why Michellian Gluttenpeals aren't a restricted species. They sound really dangerous." Solaria looked at the egg in her hands. "I don't get the feeling that this egg is harmful. It just wants to be loved." Her gaze landed on Skylar. "If I let you take it, will you bring it to me every day? Maybe we can take it up to the garden area or someplace so I can just sit and hold it. And if it starts to hatch, get me quickly." She frowned again. "This would be easier if females were allowed in the male rooms."

"Yeah it would, but even that kid—I can't remember her name—that Guppod girl that is in the middle of changing from boy to girl… anyway, she can't get in the rooms anymore. I heard her saying she went to visit her old roommates and the force field popped up to keep her in the hall. She was a little further along in her change than she thought." The event had happened in his first couple of days at school and had totally confused Skylar at the time until Del had gone into his normal explanations about how Guppods and a few other species could change sex depending on environmental conditions. As far as he was concerned, it was all perfectly natural. It sounded strange to Skylar, but he let it go. He was getting used to a lot of stranger things than boys turning into girls and vice-versa.

"Yeah, I know what you're talking about." Solaria looked happier and more relaxed than she had when they got off the school ship. "Okay. I'll let you take the egg, but you've got to bring it to me every day and as soon as it starts to hatch." She looked thoughtful. "You know, I should try and figure out a way to either get some grains or fresh meat for it, so it stays happy when it hatches."

"That might not be a bad idea," Skylar agreed. For the next couple of minutes, they discussed the egg and the possibilities it presented until the lights in the common room dimmed, indicating that the station was going into nighttime phase and they needed to vacate to their respective rooms.

Solaria slipped the egg back into her pack with a final caress before she handed the pack to Skylar. "Take care of it and return my pack tomorrow. Also, let me know if you have trouble finding somewhere comfortable for it to be. I might be able to help you make something."

Skylar nodded as he accepted the pack and carefully held it to his chest. "I'll keep that in mind. See you tomorrow."

A strange energy flowed from the egg to Skylar. It somehow reached beyond the dampening bracelet, and he wondered how powerful the baby inside the shell was. Carefully clutching it to his chest, he realized he hadn't actually touched it since Solaria took it from Pathal. Even with the dampening bracelet blocking his powers, he could still feel something inside the egg reaching out to him, like it wanted him to take care of it. He wondered if the feelings were why Solaria was so protective of it. If it was broadcasting on such a high level, how badly would it be affecting him if he didn't have his dampening bracelet on? What would happen if it proved stronger than what Solaria and Del could shield and the faculty found out? Skylar wasn't sure if that idea scared him, or excited him.

"What are you going to be, little egg?"

14
Coming Toward Center

"SO, SKYLAR, have you been doing your meditative exercises like I showed you?" Professor Aduncus asked as he removed Skylar's dampening bracelet.

Skylar didn't bother hiding his exasperated sigh. His mentor would be able to read it in his mind anyway. "I've tried. Del's been pushing me, but the calm quiet thing is something I have a lot of trouble with." It was hard to be still and introspective. Sometimes he felt he was going to come crawling out of his skin, and getting introspective made him think of his mother, and he wasn't ready for that.

Setting the bracelet on the small acrylic table where he always put it as soon as he took it off, Professor Aduncus nodded. He keyed in a code to the control panel next to the door. He did this every session, and had explained to Skylar it set up a psi dampening shield which blocked their training sessions from others on the space station and kept out any unwanted thoughts or energies that might disrupt them.

"Do you think that something more physical might help better than something calm and quiet?"

"I don't know." Skylar cocked his head at Professor Aduncus. "What sort of physical?" He wasn't sure how a physical action could help him quiet his brain. The idea seemed counterproductive.

The professor walked to the center of the empty room. "In the past, on many planets, there have always been those who found mental balance in simple physical acts. Some groups use dance."

Skylar frowned at the idea of dancing. He wasn't overly coordinated. Plus, most of the native dances on Hummassa had been fairly complex. When he watched Teir and the other kids dance at school, it had looked so beyond him. He didn't see how that could be relaxing.

Aduncus smiled. "I can tell you don't like dancing. There have also been groups who used simple martial arts to find mental balance and tranquility."

"What are martial arts?"

The professor dropped into a half-crouching position with his hands held before him. "In most sects who practice them, they are a form of fighting, but many people also see them as a style of meditation and enlightenment. Through the physical movements, as the body adjusts, the mind relaxes. For any psychic, that's the level of relaxation you're trying to achieve. Once you reach it, you'll control your mental powers. Until then, they *will* control you." Aduncus made a sweeping motion with his right hand. *"Now, join me."*

Skylar stood next to his mentor. "What do I do?"

"Simply follow my movements. I'll keep things simple for the moment. As you relax, speak with your mind, not your mouth." Professor Aduncus held his hand with its palm outward.

"I'll try." Skylar mimicked the movement. It felt easy enough.

For several minutes, he mirrored his instructor's movements. His body complained slightly at the positions he wasn't used to, but there was something simple and basic in the movements that helped him relax. When he messed up a motion, Aduncus would chuckle softly and request Skylar redo it. They finally reached a position Skylar couldn't get right.

"Why can't I do this?"

"Let us move back to the previous motion," Professor Aduncus suggested. *"That one did not give you this much trouble."*

Skylar performed the sweeping hand movement with ease.

"Good. Now, let's do this one for several minutes. The motion leads into the other one naturally."

As he went through the motion, Skylar continued to relax. The simple form began to feel good and natural. *"This really is a lot easier for me than trying to sit still and calm my mind."*

"I suspected it would be." His mentor chuckled again. *"You are not a naturally calm young man. You are more action-oriented. That is why I thought these exercises might be just what you need."*

Skylar started to nod but stopped. He'd figured out that one of the points of the exercise was to control his body, and thus control his mind. *"I am feeling much more relaxed than I have before."*

"I can tell. You don't even realize that you're speaking mind to mind with me as opposed to just hearing my thoughts."

Skylar dropped his hand in mid movement and turned to look at Professor Aduncus. "What?"

The professor smiled and lowered his own hands. "You slipped into speaking mind to mind with me as you became more relaxed. It's a very good sign. The first real progress we've seen since we began our sessions."

"But I thought I was speaking to you with my mouth." Skylar's jaw dropped. "How did I slip into mental communication with you?"

"How did you open up last month when you confronted Ms. Grissom and let the whole school know you were upset? At first, your powers react to your mental state. Last month, you were upset and they lashed out. Today, you were relaxed and they reached out very gracefully. I'd given you the suggestion that, as you relaxed, you could speak mind to mind. Your mind did just that. When we have you doing that consciously, then we'll have made our next step." Professor Aduncus dropped back into the starting stance. "We have made progress to finding your center, now let's see if you can do it again before our session ends. Begin from the start."

Skylar couldn't help but smile. With these exercises, it wasn't as hard to make progress as he had started to feel. After a month of getting nowhere, he'd began to worry. He dropped back into his own starting stance and waited for the professor to move, then mirrored his gestures and motions. When they reached the one he'd had trouble with, he did it easily but stumbled over the following move. But he didn't despair—he'd made progress—and that was something. That was enough to give him a level of hope he hadn't had when he'd entered the professor's workout room.

There was a soft knock at the door. Professor Aduncus frowned, but Skylar didn't feel any anger come from him. If his mother had been interrupted while trying to teach him something, she would've been angry.

"Continue with your exercises while I see who it is." Aduncus broke stance and walked to the door.

As Skylar went through his easy motions, sweeping his hands and body in the patterns he'd been taught, he remembered the room was shielded to not let their minds reach beyond its walls, and kept unwanted thoughts and emotions from intruding on them. He didn't doubt that if they were in Professor Aduncus' main office, he'd have known who was at the door before he opened it.

"Grandfather!" Del sounded excited. "Is Skylar with you? There is something happening and I…he should come quickly."

Skylar stopped his exercise and hurried up behind the professor. "What is it, Del?"

"Solaria wants you right away," Del blurted out. "She says it's important."

"Can I go see what she wants?" Skylar asked. "I don't think she would interrupt unless it was very important."

Aduncus sighed. There was still no anger coming from him, but there was a lot of excitement rolling off Del. "Very well. I'm pleased with your progress today. Go, see what your friend needs. I'll see you again tomorrow."

Skylar nodded. "Thank you, professor." He slid out of the room, moving quietly between his professor and the door.

He rushed alongside Del as his friend hurried away from the training room. "What's up?"

"It's too awesome, but I promised Solaria I wouldn't say anything until we got there." Del all but ran down the hall. Skylar extended his stride to keep up with him. The excitement coming off Del gave Skylar all the energy he needed, and an image of the egg kept popping into his head, pushing him faster.

15
Hatching

"WHERE'S SOLARIA?" Skylar asked as they rushed down the hall.

"She's up in the garden, near that big magnolia tree," Del replied, turning to the doorway that would take them to the inclined hall connecting the gardens and farms with the common areas. "She said she felt like the warmth of the garden would be good for the egg."

"She really does care about this egg, doesn't she?" Skylar said as several girls glared at them for rushing past, their irritation very clear even if they didn't say anything. It was after class time, and a lot of students were out meeting friends. The halls were more crowded than at any other time of the day, except maybe mornings when students were going from breakfast to class. "She normally doesn't like the garden, says it's too warm for Pantherians."

Del nodded. "Yeah. She's really fixated."

They cleared the final doors and warm, humid, earthy air hit them. It was a big enough change from the average air temperature in the halls that it took Skylar's breath away for a second. He spotted the big tree, one of the few merely ornamental ones in the garden, and his steps sped up. Even from a distance, Solaria's excitement hit him. Mingled with Del's, it made him feel almost giddy.

He stopped in front of Solaria. "What's happening?"

She beamed. "I think it's hatching." Her slitted blue eyes sparkled. "It started a few minutes ago. I was sitting here, petting it like I always do, and a pang of hunger hit me. I wondered what it meant. Then the egg shook. After the shake, the little one inside started tapping. That's when I sent Del after you. I can see where it's trying to break out of the shell." She pointed to a spot on the red and orange shell where cracks widened even as they watched.

"Wow, this is awesome." Skylar settled down on the grass next to her. "I could feel Del's excitement when he interrupted my session with his grandfather, but I wasn't sure what was going on. Thanks for sending him to get me." He looked up at Del. "And thanks for coming to get me. I wouldn't want to miss this."

Del frowned and a sense of worry hit Skylar. "Wait a minute. You don't have your dampening bracelet on, do you?"

Skylar glanced at his wrist and swore. "I must have run off so fast I forgot about it."

"Skylar, you can't be running around without it until Grandfather and Ms. Grissom say you're safe to be around other people." Del glanced around as if he expected either his grandfather or the counselor to show up and get them all in trouble. "I'll go find it. If it's not back in the training room, I'll find Grandfather and get it from him. You stay here. And whatever you do, stay calm. We don't need the whole school getting excited about this egg hatching and coming see what or who is causing the disturbance." He turned and hurried off the way they'd come.

"He is a bit of a worrywart, isn't he?" Skylar watched the egg as a small piece of shell fell away.

"Yes." Solaria sighed. "But I think he's got good reason to be. You *are getting* stronger than most of the kids around here, and caused some real trouble last time you lost control. Most level five readers couldn't be heard by the whole school, that's level seven or eight, even if they haven't said anything about it."

A pang of hunger hit Skylar as he touched the egg—it made him forget all about levels and everything else, except the little life about to come into their world. He suddenly felt like he could eat three rounds of dinner before he was full. "But this is different. This is a good thing. Nothing bad is going to happen today, is it, little egg?"

"I hope you're right. I wish we knew what was hatching. If we did, we could have food ready for it. The hunger coming off it is really strong." Solaria's stomach growled, and made Skylar wonder if she was really hungry or if the hatchling trying to escape the egg was influencing her.

"You don't think it's going to eat us as soon as it hatches, do you?"

Solaria shrugged. "That's why I wish we knew what was hatching." She looked down at the egg. "If you try to eat me, I might have to do something I really don't want to do. I'd rather be friends."

"Hey, could we try projecting thoughts and emotions at it? Maybe we can influence it. If we pour enough positive things at it, it'll have to like us, won't it?"

A wide grin crossed Solaria's face, causing her whiskers to curl up. "I like that idea! I'm only a level five feeler, but I can project a little bit. Let's try it."

"So, what's the best way to project?" Skylar stared at the egg uncertainly. "I mean, I talked mind to mind to Professor Aduncus a few minutes ago, but I'm not sure how I did it. I just relaxed and it happened." He wasn't sure he wanted to stand up and do the movements the professor showed him in public. Some of the other kids might laugh at him, and then he definitely wouldn't be able to relax enough to connect with the organism coming out of the egg.

"That's the basics of it. Just relax. Feel happy and let the emotions flow out of you and into the egg." She took a deep breath and stroked the egg. "Like this."

A strong feeling welled up from Solaria. It was like she was trying to hug him and tell him how much she cared about him. It almost felt like his mother had returned from the dead and wanted to comfort him. But since Skylar'd had a little training, he understood what she was doing. He tried to think of happy moments in his past. Visions of his mother kissing him goodnight and making him feel safe flooded up around him. He took that feeling and focused it on the egg.

Solaria nodded. "That's it. You're good at this. A natural."

Skylar touched the egg again. "Just trying to remember the good times." With everything he'd been through the past month or so, it was good to remember the happier times, before the Boarisk had attacked his home.

"Your mother was a good person," Solaria whispered. "Very pretty too."

Skylar blinked, and the quiet moment shattered. A renewed wave of hunger came from the egg. "How do you know what my mother looked like?"

"You're projecting her image right now," Solaria replied. "I can see the way she looked every night when she tucked you into bed. My mother used to do that for me too." She frowned, and longing rolled off her. "I think that's one of the things I miss the most being here at Stars' End. I miss my mother tucking me into bed every night and telling me it's going to be okay, that the shadows aren't scary."

With a deep breath, Skylar nodded. "Yeah. At least when you go home, your mother will still be there to tuck you in and make everything alright."

"I wish your mother was still alive. It would be nice to meet her. But as long as you can share your memories of her with others, a part of her will still be here." Solaria took Skylar's hand in hers. Her stubby fingers felt velvety soft against his skin. "Tell you what. Maybe if things get too intense for either of us, we can share stories of our mothers and remember the good times."

Skylar swallowed and tried to find his voice. "That would be nice."

In Solaria's lap, the egg shook violently. The small crack widened. A tiny yellow snout pushed its way out of the shell.

Del came rushing up, breathless. He had the dampening bracelet in his hand. "Here it is. Did I miss anything?" He stopped and stared down at the little nose poking out of the shell. "Well, it's definitely not a bird."

Solaria shook her head. "Nope, not a bird. I think we're going to need meat for it."

A very high-pitched squeak came from the little yellow snout. It gasped for breath before emitting another squeak.

"I bet it's calling for its mother," Del said.

"And we don't know how to reply," Solaria stared down at the egg in her lap as little pieces of red and orange shell fell onto her gray pants.

It let out another squeak.

Del knelt down next to Skylar and in front of Solaria. "Let me try to mimic it. Tursiops can hit some pretty high notes." The squeak he made was similar to the thing hatching from the egg. It gave another squeak and struggled against the shell.

"Skylar, why don't you and I keep broadcasting at it while Del continues encouraging it?" Solaria suggested.

Hope and excitement poured off her, making it hard for Skylar to tell which were her emotions and which his, but in that moment, it didn't matter. "Once it's free and if it doesn't try to eat us, I'll run and get some raw meat for it."

"Okay." Using the same feelings and images as before, Skylar tried to make the little hatchling feel welcome.

As his energies melded with Solaria's and Del continued to squeak at it, the little yellow snout pushed further out of the egg, dropping more shell fragments into Solaria's lap. The rest of the head appeared, sleek and reptilian. Bright orange eyes looked at the three of them.

"I think it's a Solar Drake!" Del said, his eyes wide.

"Then it's not going to try and eat us," Solaria replied.

Seconds later, it had enough of the egg broken away that it could force its way free of the rest. Once clear of the eggshell, it collapsed in Solaria's lap.

"Is it dead?" Skylar stared down at the delicate yellow wings with orange and red lines decorating them. The little body looked like some of the lizards he'd played with in the jungles of Hummassa, but beyond the basic shape, most lizards didn't have long wings and bright orange eyes. He hoped they weren't supposed to have been feeding it as it came out of the shell, and by not doing so had killed the little guy.

"I can still feel it's alive," Solaria said. "We need to feed it. Now!"

"I'll get some fish from the stream," Del offered. "That'll be fastest."

Skylar looked at his friend. "But you don't have a net or fishing pole."

Del stood. "I don't need one." He ran off toward the stream that cut through the center of the garden.

"I didn't know he could fish." Skylar turned his attention back to the little Solar Drake as Solaria picked it up.

"All Tursiops can fish. It's part of what they evolved for," she explained without looking at him. It took both of her hands to hold the little lizard, and its wings still drooped over her fingers.

"So, now what do we do with it?" Skylar asked. He stopped himself from reaching out to touch it.

"First we feed it, then you and Del take it back to your room and keep it safe there until we have more time to think." She sounded sad.

"Why our room?"

Solaria looked up at him. The frown on her face confirmed her sadness. "I did some research on the list of things Del said could come out of the egg. Solar Drakes, especially young ones, do best in either human standard or higher temperatures. The planet they come from is tropical. This little one would not do well in my room. It's too cold." She moved her thumb in small circular motions against its side. "I wish I could take it back with me, but I shouldn't. I don't think it would do well even if I called my folks and had them come get it."

Skylar stared at the Solar Drake. "So… now what?" He was beginning to understand Solaria's urge to protect the little thing. It was so small and delicate. It definitely needed them to watch over it.

Del returned before Solaria could say anything else. "Here, it's not a big fish, but I think it might be enough to get him started eating." The shiny silver fish dangling from his fingers was about half the size of the hatchling.

"That should do." Solaria nodded. "Now, cut it into little pieces so we can get them into its mouth."

"But we don't have a knife," Skylar pointed out.

"Here, hold it for me." Solaria gently thrust the little yellow drake at him. It opened its eyes and squeaked at him.

Skylar put his hands under hers and she deposited the hatchling in them. It didn't weigh much, about half the weight of the egg. It looked up at Skylar and, as the orange eyes looked into his blue ones, he knew he'd do anything to keep it safe and make sure it had a home. It was very precious and very special.

"Little one, do you want some fish?" Solaria asked as she held a piece of fish on her claw near the hatchling's mouth.

The tiny yellow nostrils flared and its head flashed around and grabbed the meat. It gulped it down, and then looked back up at Skylar.

"I think he likes it." Skylar smiled. He took it as a good sign that it was eating. The better it ate, the more chance it had to survive.

Solaria offered it another piece, which it gulped right down like the other. "I think you're right. Let's see if it will eat all of this fish."

"I can get more if I need to," Del offered. "They keep the stream really well stocked and I doubt anyone's going to miss a few minnows and such."

"Let's get this one in it first," Solaria replied without looking at him as she gave the baby drake another piece of fish.

Within a couple of minutes, the fish was gone. The little drake circled around Skylar's cupped hands, folded its wings over its back, then tucked its head under one wing and went to sleep. A feeling of contentment spread over Skylar as he sat there in the grass with the little lizard asleep in his hand. *He's depending on me. I've got to do right by him.*

"Do you want more fish?" Del asked.

"Let him sleep for now," Solaria said. "We'll sneak some meat out of the kitchen so you and Skylar can feed him later." The look she gave the little one reminded Skylar of the looks his mother would give him when she tucked him in for the night. It was the look that told him that everything was going to be okay.

Del fidgeted next to them. "How do you know it's a he?"

Solaria shrugged. "Feels like a boy to me. Can't really explain it."

Del huffed. "Sometimes I wish I was stronger, psychically speaking."

"But you're smart," Skylar said, not liking the wave of sadness coming off Del. Then he remembered he wasn't wearing the dampening bracelet. "Hey, can you put my bracelet back on for me?" He held his arm out to Del. "I guess I don't need to go around picking up every little thought and feeling from everyone."

"Ah." Del fished the bracelet out of his pocket. "I can't believe we still forgot to put this back on you."

"A lot's been going on," Solaria added as Del snapped the bracelet in place, instantly quieting the thoughts and emotions hitting Skylar.

The little Solar Drake in his other hand squirmed suddenly but didn't wake. It squeaked twice, then stilled. Skylar looked at it and couldn't help but smile. "What are we going to call him?"

Solaria shook her head. "We probably shouldn't name him. We've got to try to get him home. He doesn't belong here. If we give him a name, giving him up will be a lot harder when the time comes."

Looking at the small ball of yellow and orange in his hands, Skylar wasn't sure he wanted to get rid of him, but it was the logical thing to do.

"I agree. But we're going to have to come up with a good plan. These little guys are a restricted species and most of the information on them is classified," Dell said, putting his hands under his legs so he was sitting on them.

"And how did you get the information?" Solaria licked her claws clean of fish guts.

"Dark web. When the normal sources didn't come up with a whole lot, I went digging elsewhere." Del continued to fidget. "I can't tell where all of it's coming from, but there's a lot of information being dumped out there right now on Solar Drakes."

"I wonder if the people who stole this egg in the first place are putting out the information," Skylar pondered. He desperately wanted to pet the little drake, but resisted, thinking it was probably better to let it sleep after its first meal.

"That could be. An increased interest in them might create a black market for them." Del pulled his hands out from under his legs and began to drum on his thigh. It was something he did when he was thinking. "One of the posts I read the other night said that when they bind with a psychic, they can take a low level psi and make them stronger. Weaker people might really be interested in them once that information gets out."

Skylar didn't like the fact that the information was off the dark web. He'd never had any cause to go there and get data, but he'd always heard the people who posted things there weren't the best people in the universe. They had their own agendas for everything they did. He didn't want unscrupulous people getting their hands on Solar Drakes, but if their egg had gotten off the planet, then others might have as well. It made him nervous, and more determined to get the little guy home safe and sound.

16
The Box

SKYLAR DRIED his hands and hurried out of the bathroom toward the cafeteria. This past week, he'd spent a lot of time washing his hands. The little Solar Drake needed raw meat, which left bloody streaks on his fingers. He was just thankful that Solaria managed to get the meat. He didn't know how, and really didn't care as long as she kept the supply coming. The little drake was growing and Skylar enjoyed taking care of it. It felt good having something that looked to him for comfort and care.

Del sat staring droopily at his table when Skylar set his lunch tray on the table next to him. Skylar looked at Solaria. "What's with him?"

She shrugged as she lifted another fork of meat to her mouth. "Not sure, he's not said anything since I sat down. He's just engrossed in his tablet," she replied after swallowing.

Confused by his friend's strange attitude, Skylar mixed the gravy into his mashed potatoes before trying the direct approach. "Del, what's going on?"

"Spatial navigation," Del muttered. "My worst class. I'm making a solid three-point-oh in it. I just don't understand why I can't get a better grip of the principles. Sure, it's complex physics, but it shouldn't be this hard."

Skylar chewed a mouthful of fresh peas before answering. He'd known other really smart kids over the years who got upset about getting grades he'd be thrilled to have. It always made him stop and scratch his head.

"So, what don't you understand? Not that I know much about spatial navigation yet. The class here is the first time I've been exposed to most of it, but isn't the hardest part making sure you don't fly into a black hole or through the heart of a sun?"

Del rolled his eyes. "Not exactly. You've got to make sure everything's in alignment. You can't get too close to most planets or you risk having your course affected by their gravity wells. It even applies to large asteroids. There are all kinds of things that can throw a ship off course. Miss an adjustment by even a *fraction* of a second and you lose the ship. In my last simulation, I couldn't get a simple shuttle run from one planet to another to work out right."

"That's why you hire a good pilot," Solaria said, finished off her meat and starting on a large piece of what Skylar thought was a fruit, but couldn't be sure. "Make sure he or she made a higher grade than you did in navigation and the problem's solved."

Del's frown intensified. "But that doesn't help me with the class. I've got to get great grades to get a good position after school. You'll be hired by someone needing a marginal mover, so you're assured of a decent job. I'm not—unless I've got the grades to back up my brains." He set the tablet down and glared at his uneaten lunch like it was something horrible and he wasn't about to touch it.

Before Del could do anything, Ms. Grissom appeared at their table carrying a small black plastic shipping box. "Skylar, this just arrived in the mail. It's addressed to you, but there isn't any return destination. I queried the mail bot about it, and its records are incomplete on this one parcel. Since we respect our student's privacy, I felt it wise to bring it to you, but I would like you to open it with me here, just in case you need my professional counseling." She handed him the box.

Hoping he wasn't going to need any of her *professional* skills, Skylar looked at the box in his hands. "If you're that worried about how I'm going to react, why not pull me into your office again?" He didn't bother trying to hide his irritation. One of the lessons he was rapidly learning about dealing with the various psychics in the academy was that it wasn't worth the effort trying to hide things. Even though he had his dampening bracelet on, she would still be able to pick up on the small tell-tale signs of emotions on his face.

Ms. Grissom didn't react. "You need to learn to control yourself better in public. This is an excellent opportunity."

He took the box from her. Using the dull plastic knife from his lunch, he managed to get the packing seal broken so he could lift the flaps and expose the contents. Inflatable cushions held two things away from the box's sides. It took almost as much effort to break through the cushions as it had the seal.

The cushions sighed as air escaped. Once they were completely deflated, Skylar reached in and pulled out the larger of the two items. It looked much like a small tablet, but there was a small connector port on one side, right next to what Skylar hoped was the power button.

The device lit up just like a tablet would.

"Hey, that's cool." Del peered over Skylar's shoulder.

"Okay, what is it? It looks like a cross between a tablet and a power com." Skylar turned it over and couldn't find any markings on the back side of the thing.

"That's exactly what it is," Del said. "The coms we use rely on a larger com system to make them work." He held up his hand, where his white dermal com clashed with the gray skin there. Then he pointed at the device.

"That's a Power Com Thirty-Six Hundred. No matter where you are in the galaxy, it'll be able to connect you to the Galactic Communications Network." He held out his hand asking silently to see it. "They rely on the stargate network to transmit messages, not satellites."

Skylar handed it over. "And what good does that thing do me? It's not like we're going to get off the station or out of the range of a ship where our communicators work."

"Yeah, but these things aren't cheap," Del explained. "It's last year's model, too."

Solaria snatched it out of Del's hand. She stared at it for a couple of seconds before handing it back to him. "It's also somewhat used."

Del looked at it some more before handing it back to Skylar. "How can you tell it's used?"

She sighed. "I'm a predator. I notice little things, like the slight wear on the power button and the tiny scratch in the upper left-hand corner of the screen. Definite signs of wear. Light wear, but wear none the less."

Skylar frowned. Someone sent him a used com and he had no idea who or why.

Del stared into the box. "What's the other thing?"

"Don't know." Skylar reached into the box and pulled out a smaller silver cube. It was small enough for him to hold in his palm. There were a series of buttons on it. He touched one and a small screen appeared on the side. A slideshow flashed on the screen. They were pictures of tools.

Skylar tapped the screen when the picture of a pair of scissors appeared. The little box shook, folded in on itself several times, and then there was a small pair of scissors sitting in Skylar's palm.

"Incredible," Del said. "That's a Swiss multi-tool. It can be anything you need it to be in the way of tools. Wow, someone really likes you."

Ms. Grissom frowned. "I'm not sure I should let you have that. It could be disruptive. I could hold it for you until you graduate."

"Oh, come on, Ms. Grissom," Solaria said. "He hasn't got anything for himself that isn't school issue. Let him keep it. Besides, it's just a little multi-tool. How much damage can he do with it? Anything he might break, the repair bots will have fixed before faculty can find out about it—that is, if the tool doesn't help him fix it faster than the bots can."

"You know," Del chimed in, "I bet Grandfather will vouch for him on this. Let him keep it."

The counselor looked at Skylar. "Do you want to keep it?"

Skylar looked down at the silver pair of scissors sitting in his hand. He tapped the black rivet that joined the two halves together. The blades shook like the box had before and after a few folds, it was back to its original shape. He had no idea who'd sent it, but it was really kinda awesome. And it would be his. The little Solar Drake wasn't completely his. He shared the pet with Del and Solaria, and they were planning on finding a way to get it home, so it wouldn't be theirs for long. "Yes." He nodded. "I think I do want to keep it. It's incredible. I wish we knew who sent it."

The frown stayed on Ms. Grissom's face. "Very well. But if I get any reports of you misusing either item, I *will* be forced to take them from you until you graduate from Stars' End. Do I make myself clear?"

"Yes, ma'am." Skylar nodded. Even though he wanted to stay on good terms with everyone, he still wanted to keep the multi-tool. It was something he could call his own.

"Okay. Have a good day." Ms. Grissom turned and left.

"Wow, this is great." Del's droopy face was gone as he picked up the com. "I wonder who sent you these things?"

"Probably the same person that paid for my tuition," Skylar said, flipping through the images on the little screen. He'd never dreamed there were so many different tools, or that one thing could become all of them. "I'd like to know why. And if he's going to send me this stuff, why not just come and say hello?" An idea hit him. "Del, do you think maybe you could see if you can find anything interesting on it?"

"Yeah, maybe there's a message of some sort on the com unit," Solaria suggested. "If there is, I'm sure Del can find it." She stood and picked up her tray. "But right now, it's almost time for next class. This afternoon, let's take the little guy up to the garden. He could probably use some sunshine for a little while."

Slipping the tool into his pocket, Skylar nodded. "Sounds like a plan. See you then." He finally had something of his own. After he'd heard his home had been destroyed in the Boarisk attack, it was nice to have something he could hold and call his. It was yet another way to get back to feeling like normal.

17
Z-GBall

SKYLAR STROLLED down the hall, heading with Del to their last class of the day. "Have you made any headway in your navigation problem?"

Del sighed dramatically. "No. I don't know what to do. I get the basic idea. I've watched every beginning and intermediate video I can find on it, but so far, I just can't wrap my mind around the more delicate maneuvering. It's not like I'm planning on getting my own ship some day or anything; I just don't want the lower class score to bring down my average."

"Look out! Coming through!" Solaria pushed between them.

"Hey, what's happening?" Skylar rushed after her, Del's navigation problem momentarily forgotten.

"Don't have time right now. I've got less than two hours to practice." She didn't break stride as she maneuvered through a couple of older students who shot her harsh looks as she scooted by them.

"But aren't you heading for art class with Del and me?" Skylar ignored the glares they received as he somehow managed to keep up with her.

Solaria shook her head. "I've already let Mr. Hemsbely know that I won't be there today. This is more important."

They headed up the ramp leading to the center of the space station. "Okay, but what is it?"

"A Z-GBall game. First one this year and I'm on the defending team." She paused and turned to him. Skylar couldn't remember seeing her so excited since the egg hatched. "Look, you've got time for art class and to feed the hatchling. Del will know where to get the best seats for the match. You guys better be there to cheer me on." Her voice was low, barely audible.

"Oh, don't worry, we'll be there." Del appeared, slightly breathless, at Skylar's side. "I never miss a Z-GBall match."

Solaria nodded. "Good. I'll look for you." Then she dashed off.

"THIS STILL sounds really complicated," Skylar said as he and Del hurried from their room after feeding the hatchling and cleaning up.

Del shrugged. "It is and it isn't. The point of the game is to get as many points as possible while not using jet packs to maneuver in the zero-gravity center of the station. Anyone who uses jet packs ends up having a point deducted for each use."

"But the balls respond to… psychic energy?" As they entered the main hall that ran toward the ramp for the gardens on the inner surface of the station, Skylar realized that most of the students—and a few teachers— were also heading that way. It was the most crowded he'd ever seen the area.

"Yeah, but that's a fairly recent addition to the games," Del continued as they cleared the press of people and headed for a lift. "One of the professors came up with the psi-balls a few years ago. It's made the game a lot more interesting. Some people think that some of the balls used have a kind of rudimentary intelligence that responds to the emotions of the players. They actually seem to attack the more aggressive ones. During a game last year, a mid-level feeler got super mad during the game, and the ball hit him really hard several times. He ended up in the med center for a couple of days."

Skylar's eyes grew wide. He wasn't sure he liked the idea of a game where the balls could become aggressive. Sounded dangerous, but it might be a good reminder for everyone to keep their tempers while playing. "Wow, and they actually let students play this game?"

"Play?" Del chuckled. "Students invented Z-GBall. It's how we settle conflicts. While you were feeding the little one, I did some checking. The station intranet is all abuzz. It turns out that Kril Mctunia insulted Felicianana Palas this morning over breakfast. She gave him the option of a Z-GBall game, or she could put him down in the cafeteria. Since a game involves a team, it gives him the opportunity to claim someone else is at fault if his team loses. But if you ask me, I think folks have just been looking for an excuse for a game. It's always interesting to see who ends up on which team. The two people involved get to pick and it's usually different each time."

"And how long does the game go on?" Skylar asked as they waited for the lift.

"When the first team gets a hundred points, they stop the game." The lift arrived and they got in. "If the two teams are less than twenty-five points apart, they continue until there is a decisive winner."

Skylar shook his head as the lift shot off. Once it cleared the first floor up, Skylar realized that the walls were transparent, and when it passed into the garden section, the view was amazing. He'd been so busy, he hadn't thought to explore the whole station. There were still parts he hadn't discovered. Through the clear barrier above them, he could just barely make out the small forms of ten people maneuvering in the zero gravity area that existed in the very center of the station. "Twenty-five points isn't decisive?"

"Nope. I don't know who came up with the figure. I guess it might be because since the games are mostly used to settle differences, they want to make sure the losers know and really feel that they've lost."

The people in the garden area all appeared to be looking either at their wrist coms or various tablets. Very few of them watched the people floating above them.

"It does sound a bit humiliating losing by more than twenty-five points."

"Hey, there was a game last year, some of the corp-brats versus the Cryptods. The corp-brats used their jetpacks so much that when the Cryptods hit a hundred points, the corp-brats only had five. Now *there* was a decisive victory." The lift slowed as it passed through the protective barrier that defined the zero-gravity area. The gravity in the lift faded. "By the way, we have to help out with the scoring, but I got us really good seats for the game."

Skylar stared at the panorama unfolding around them as he began to float. "Help with the scoring? What do I know about scoring?" He was just learning about the game. It didn't seem like he was going to be able to do a decent job with scoring.

Del moved closer to the lift doors, grabbing hold of a silver rail there. "It's easy. You'll be assigned a player, and you just keep track of how many times they use their jetpack."

"Don't they use the computer for this?" Skylar asked as the lift stopped. He pushed himself off the back of the lift to grab the rail alongside Del.

"It was deemed that there was too much of an opportunity for cheating if computers were used, so way back in time, they opted for a sentient count as backup." Del floated through the doors as they slid open. "If the stories are true, one of the team captains hacked into the scoring computer and the team ended up getting two points for every actual point they scored, while the opposing team suffered a five-point penalty every time they used their jetpacks. But regardless of what really happened, people are the scorekeepers now."

On the other side of the lift doors was a medium-sized booth with a large number of monitors and holographic screens. There were nine people in the room, most seated at separate monitors. In the center of the room floated one of the snail-like Pulmonians in its envirobubble.

One of its eye stalks swiveled toward them. "Del, glad you could make it. Since there are Tursiops playing, are you sure that you can be objective?" A speaker on the outside of the envirobubble projected its voice to them.

Del nodded enthusiastically. "Sure, Monte. I don't have anything riding on this game." From the way he moved in the weightless environment, Skylar knew Del had a fair amount of experience at it, but then wondered if being weightless was a lot like being in an ocean.

Skylar watched the ten people floating about, moving easily, either by jetpack or swinging from the rails that ran along the sides of the clear barrier that showed the gardens. Solaria seemed to fly around without any aid whatsoever. He wished he could move so easily. He kept grabbing various consoles, rails, and workstations to get further into the booth.

"And your friend? Is he neutral?" Monte drew Skylar's attention away from the players and back to the beings in the control room.

Skylar turned back to Monte but kept a firm grip on the back of an empty chair. "I'm new here. Can't get much more neutral than that."

"And you're human, so you probably can be neutral with Pantherian or Tursiop as a whole. That's only logical. Okay, there are two more terminals. You sit next to Del—he can help if there's any problem. I trust he's already explained how the game works?"

"Yeah." Skylar nodded. "I think I understand." He tried to sound more confident than he felt. His stomach kept knotting at the idea of missing something important and screwing up with everyone counting on him to be impartial.

Monte shifted in his envirobubble. "We've got three minutes folks. Get ready."

Skylar glanced at Del, trying to figure out what Monte meant by nuetral.

Del shook his head. "No, I'm a great shielder and Skylar's got a dampening bracelet on right now."

He glanced at Skylar and gestured for him to raise his arm. When Monte saw the bracelet, his eyestalks bounced in what Skylar could only assume was a nod.

"Two-minute warning!" Monte announced. In the game area below, everyone lined up.

Del gestured for Skylar to follow him to the two empty monitors. It took Skylar nearly a full minute to make it to the chair Del indicated. He was pleasantly surprised to find a seat belt that would keep him in place. As they got seated, the monitors came to life.

"Okay"—Del leaned over to Skylar—"now see the image on the screen, that's who you're keeping track of. Oh hey, that's Felicianana Palas. The screen will show you what's going on, but you concentrate on her. Every time she uses her jet pack, you tap the red button there." He gestured to the large red button on the lower right of the screen. "That's all you've got to do."

Skylar nodded. "That sounds easy enough." As long as he didn't hit the button by mistake, everything should be great.

"It can be, but sometimes you get so wrapped up in the game, you might forget. Try not to. It'll look bad for both of us." Del settled back into his own seat.

"One minute!" Monte called.

Even with the dampening bracelet blocking his abilities, the tension in the room was palpable. Monte floated to the edge of the booth. He touched a button with one of his eyestalks, and a ball shot into the zero-gravity playing field. The players all seemed to be in motion at once. Felicianana and Solaria both took off toward the ball. For the first time, it registered with Skylar that they carried long rods. Solaria swung her rod at the ball. Her swing was true and the ball flew off into the floating blue cube that was the Tursiops goal as she tumbled backward. The ring of white light around the goal hole flashed red as the goal floated off to a new position, slightly lower than it had been.

"First goal, Solaria for the Pantherians!" Monte announced. The distant sound of cheering came from speakers set near the lift.

Skylar kept his cheer silent, and was thankful he had the dampening bracelet on so no one in the booth could feel his excitement that his friend scored the first goal of the game.

A small burst of white came from Felicianana's jetpack as the compressed air propelled her toward the ball that came hurling out of the goalbot. Skylar tapped the red button and a one appeared next to it.

One of the Tursiops swung off a rail and shot toward the ball. He barely missed Felicianana and managed to hit the ball further into Pantherian territory. Again, Solaria moved forward without any obvious help. One of the other Pantherians kicked off the goal toward the ball, but a Tursiops that appeared to be moving the same way as Solaria got there faster. He hit the ball. It didn't go anywhere, but *he* tumbled end over end toward the barrier. Felicianana swooped down faster than Solaria and hit the ball. It flew back toward the Tursiops goal.

"That's always hard when that happens," Del said as he tapped the red button on his screen.

"What was that?" Skylar asked.

"That was the ball having a mind of its own. Well, that and partially a zero-gravity thing. For every action, there is an equal and opposite reaction. That's why when folks hit the ball they get thrown off course, even the ones using telekinesis, like Solaria. They're still affected by the basic rules of physics in the environment out there."

"Score, Felicianana for the Pantherians!" Monte's voice echoed through the speakers.

Felicianana propelled herself off the goal and floated to the middle of the field. The ball returned to play. Solaria soared past a Tursiops heading for the ball, but Felicianana already had it coming back toward the Tursiops goal. One of the Tursiops flew toward the ball. He missed his swing, but the ball caught him in the gut. The impact sent him flying toward the control booth. He hit the clear barrier hard.

"Break. We need a med bot in the field to remove the injured player!" Monte shouted. "From what I can tell, he's going to be unconscious for at least an hour. That was some hit. But it's a hard blow for Kril. Flip was his best player."

Skylar glanced at Del. "How long is the break?"

"Until the med bot gets Flip off the field," Del explained. "We can't have injured players floating around getting in the way. School rules. They used to be left in the area till the school changed the rules, and now we have to get them to safety."

A small white and red remote-controlled bot appeared from an alcove further down the field. Little white puffs of air accompanied it as it maneuvered toward the unconscious Flip.

Skylar looked out onto the field. "Are there often injured players?" All the players were still where they had been when the break was called. Even the ball and goals were frozen in space.

"Every so often. Like I said on the way over here, if the ball doesn't like you, it can be a lot worse. I don't think that's what occurred with Flip. He just caught a bad blow. It happens."

"If you say so."

The med bot latched onto Flip's floating form and dragged him toward the alcove adjacent to the announcer's booth. Beyond the alcove, a medical team waited.

Once the bot slipped back into the alcove, Monte sighed. "Okay, let's get this going again," he said at a normal volume before calling, "Resume play!"

The players all moved at once. Those who weren't close enough to kick off something used their jetpacks to get going again. Skylar hit the red button to yank another point from Felicianana.

The game settled into a fairly predictable rhythm. After an hour, the Pantherians had seventy-five points and the Tursiops had forty. Solaria and the Tursiops mover appeared to have an advantage over the other players. They didn't have any penalty points for using their jet packs, although Skylar noticed the Tursiops mover seemed to be tiring as the game continued, while Solaria maintained her speed and agility. The two movers had scored more points than any of the others on the field.

Something distracted the Tursiops mover just as the ball flew in his direction. He swung his rod and missed. Right before the ball would've caught him in the head, he used his jetpack to get out of its way. The ball caught him in the foot and sent him tumbling.

The Pantherians heightened their aggression. Within minutes, Skylar was fairly sure they had just been toying with their rival team. It only took them fifteen minutes to drive their score up to a hundred.

"Well, that's a game folks!" Monte called out. "The score is Felicianana and the Pantherians, one hundred, Kril and the Tursiops twenty. Better luck next time Kril."

The cheering from the speakers reached a fever pitch. Even with the dampening bracelet on, it hit Skylar hard. A surge of joy and happiness stronger than anything he'd ever felt before made him almost giddy.

"Thanks for the help, folks," Monte said. "You all did a great job, even the new guy. If you want to monitor the next game, I'll get in touch when it gets scheduled."

A round of "Sure," "Anytime," and "Count me in!" rang out in the booth. Then everyone started for the lift.

About halfway down, Del's com beeped. He glanced at it. "Skylar, we've got to get back to the room as fast as we can. The alarm just went off."

"What alarm?" They couldn't move any faster— there were a lot of people around them.

"I set up an alarm after you brought *it* in," Del whispered. "Just in case something happened when we weren't there. I was afraid Panthal might try something, or that something else might happen. Well, something just did."

Skylar's heart pounded. *Please let the little guy be alright.* He wished he could get out of the lift right then. When the door opened, he pushed his way through the doors and dashed toward their room. He didn't even bother seeing if Del followed him or not.

18
Separation Anxiety

A LOUD crash filled the nearly empty hallway as Skylar ran toward his room. He skidded to a stop and pressed his palm against the bioscanner that locked their door. The portal reluctantly slid open to reveal a scene of chaos.

The beds were trashed. Everything that had been on a desk or shelf now lay on the floor. Clothes were scattered about, worse than normal. Fear filled the room, breaking through Skylar's bracelet. That hit him harder than the mess that filled the room.

"What happened here?"

"Hold the door!" Del charged up behind him. "What happened here?"

Skylar glanced at his friend. "That's what I just asked."

Del frowned at the door. "Someone tried to break in. I bet it was Pathal. With everyone down at the game, he and his bottom feeders must've thought it was a good time to try to get the egg back."

Something flung itself out from under the nearest pile of clothes. A bright yellow and orange streak flew at Skylar. He barely got his arm up before the hatchling landed on him. His bright, multi-colored eyes sparkled and a feeling of surprise and happiness rolled off it. It reached out and preened a bit of Skylar's hair.

"Did you do all this?" he asked.

The little Solar Drake stared back at him, then rubbed his head against his hand before making the soft, almost purring sound that Skylar recognized as a request for food.

Del pushed Skylar far enough into the room that the door could close. "We need to get this place cleaned up. Fin and Connor are not going to be happy to see it trashed like this."

Skylar looked at the drake. "But why would he do something like this? Did Pathal or whoever make it and scare him? And when did he start flying?"

"I don't know, but he can obviously fly now." Del bent over and picked up a shirt. "This looks like yours."

"Toss it on my bed." Skylar gestured to the center of the destruction in the room as he continued to stare at the drake. "What are we going to do with you while we try and get you back home?" He glanced at the door, a feeling of dread settling in his stomach. If Pathal had finally gotten the nerve to try to recover the egg, would he try again? Or would the alarm Del put on the place be enough to dissuade him from doing anything else in the future?

Tossing more of Skylar's clothes onto the growing pile, Del sighed. "I think we need Solaria in on this discussion. If we make a decision about him without her, then we'll be in trouble."

Stroking the drake's little head, Skylar nodded. "I think you're right there, but what kind of decision can we make?"

Del frowned. "He's obviously growing up. Pretty soon, someone—beyond the few people that already know—is going to find out. I bet it's not going to go well. We've also got to ask ourselves if it's right to keep him locked up in this room all the time. From what I've been able to find out, it's going to take a bit to get the right permits to get him home."

"But we take him out to the garden with us at least once a day." Skylar shifted the drake to his shoulder and started helping Del pick up. The longer he had the drake, the more he wondered about taking him back to Armstrong's Ring, the planet where the drakes lived. He was getting more and more fond of him.

"Yeah, in a pack. How long before he starts complaining about that? And we're just really lucky that nobody's caught us when we're out in the garden." Del stopped moving things about and tapped his com. "Solaria Uncia. Hey Solaria, can you come to our room? The little guy's started flying and trashed the place. Also we're wondering if Pathal tried to break in."

Skylar couldn't make out the response since Del hadn't opted to share the com with him. But Del's face didn't change. It still had a dark worried look. "Okay, see you in a few." He looked at Skylar. "She's not happy that we're interrupting her after-game celebration, but she'll be here in a few."

"Okay." Skylar set some books up on his desk. For the next few minutes, with the little drake shifting on his shoulder for balance, Skylar worked on putting the room back together

They had a fair semblance of order when Connor showed up.

"What happened in here?" their roommate demanded.

"The little guy's learning to fly," Skylar said quickly, trying to make it sound like a good thing. He opted to not say anything about the possible break in and hoped neither Connor nor Fin would notice the slight slowness in the way their door slid open.

Connor frowned. "He better not break any of my stuff."

Del shook his head. "It doesn't look like anything got broken. I think he's just being a bit clumsy is all. He'll get better at it."

"You better hope so." Connor stomped over to his desk and glared at the pile of knick-knacks there. He held up an antique book and glared at Skylar and the drake on his shoulder. "Look at this!" He pointed at fresh scratch marks on it. "I can't fix this. It's a very valuable family heirloom. Keep him away from my stuff." Connor slammed the book into a drawer and set about organizing his area.

"Sorry, Connor." Skylar started to give an extended apology, but, by the way their roommate slammed things back into their proper place, Connor probably wasn't interested in hearing it.

Someone knocked on their door. "Skylar, Del, it's Solaria."

"We'll be right out." Skylar dug his pack out from under the pile of clothes on his bed and motioned the little drake inside. "Come on, we'll get out of here for a bit." As it had done for nearly a week, the hatchling walked into the pack. Skylar didn't bother closing it before slipping it over his shoulder and following Del to the door. He felt a sense of relief getting away from Connor's justifiable anger.

As the door opened, Solaria gestured at the door frame. "Looks like someone tried to pry it open. The door was a couple seconds slower moving than normal." She tapped a couple of scrapes that marred the gray metal of the frame, then peered into the room.

"What!" Connor shouted.

She appeared to ignore him. "Wow, our little guy made that mess?" A wide smile crossed her face. "He's going to be a bit of a handful, huh."

Del frowned. "Going to be? He already is. We need to figure out what we're going to do about this—and soon. While we're at it, I could use some food and he sounds hungry… again."

"Food sounds awesome," Skylar agreed. They hadn't gotten themselves anything to eat before the game, although he and Del had fed the hatchling.

"Tell you what." Solaria pointed a finger emphatically. "Skylar, you take the little guy and go to the garden. The crowds are mostly moving to the cafeteria. I'll run get some food for him and Del can get some for the rest of us."

Skylar nodded. "That works for me."

They went their separate ways. Inside the pack, the little drake squirmed a bit, then settled into a comfortable lump against Skylar's left side. Having the drake there next to him made Skylar relax.

As he walked down the hall, he reached into the pack and rubbed the little yellow head. There were tiny knots just beginning to push their way out of his leathery skin. They made him wonder if the little guy was starting to grow horns, and he promised himself to look closer at him when he got to the garden.

The magnolia tree they liked to sit in—and under— was empty when he got there. Like Solaria said, most of the students had left the garden already, and the few that hadn't were either absorbed in their personal activities, or on their way out when Skylar arrived.

As soon as he reached the tree, he opened up the pack and the drake dashed out and scurried up into the tree. He walked out onto the lowest branch and spread his yellow wings. The orange veins in his wings blazed almost red in the light. *I bet that would be really pretty in a bright sunset,* Skylar thought as he looked up at the drake. *He really is the greatest thing I've ever seen. And those do look like little horns coming up above his eye ridges.*

"Okay, here we go." Solaria appeared with a cup that Skylar knew would have raw meat for the hatchling in it. "Where is he?"

Skylar pointed up to the low branch in the tree. "He ran up there as soon as I opened the pack. He's getting a lot more active."

Solaria nodded as she pulled out a little piece of meat. "Yeah, little ones don't stay little long. But I'd hoped he'd be small for more than a week or so. His wings are definitely getting bigger. Are those horns growing on his head?" She held up the piece of meat. The hatchling launched himself off the branch and glided down to her for it. She smiled. Her whiskers rose and her blue eyes sparkled. "That's it, little one. Did you trash the guys' room 'cause you're learning how to fly, or did you get scared?"

The Solar Drake gulped the meat down and looked at her with an expression that Skylar now recognized as "More!"

"Let's see if we can get him to fly between us." Solaria thrust the cup of meat to Skylar. He grabbed a piece and held it out in his palm, his hand just far enough away from Solaria that the little drake would have to jump or fly to get it.

For a moment, the drake's serpentine gaze shifted between the cup of meat in her hand and the meat lying in Skylar's open palm. Then he flapped his growing wings and flew to Skylar. A giddy feeling of joy spread through him. Having the tiny feet land on his hand when he was expecting it made him happy, not like the bolt of fear and surprise when it had come out of his clothes at him in his room. "Great!"

"Let's do that again." Solaria pulled out another piece of meat and stepped back from Skylar. "Maybe we can help him build up his wing muscles. That would be good. We want him to grow up big and strong for when we get him home."

She held out her hand with the meat visible. The drake flew easily between them. It was something very simple, but it still made Skylar feel great. Their little hatchling was now a fledgling. On the third flight to Solaria, it dove under her hand and grabbed the cup with the food.

"Hey!" she fussed. "That's not how we play this game."

The little drake finished off the meat in the cup in three big gulps, then hopped up to her hand and scarfed down the piece there. Solaria laughed as Del arrived with their food.

"What did I miss?" Del asked as he set three small, clear boxes on the ground before sitting down between them.

Skylar sat next to Del as Solaria settled across from him. "We had the little guy fly between us to feed him. He liked it, until he figured out he could eat all the meat out of the cup at one time instead of waiting for us to offer it to him."

"He's really cute with his flying." Solaria stroked the little drake, running her finger from his head all the way down to his tail.

"I hate to keep harping on this but we really need to figure out what we're going to do with him." Del handed a box to Skylar. "If he's going to be more mobile, he's going to get noticed a lot more easily. I also don't know if Connor and Fin are going to help us hide him if he keeps trashing the room."

Solaria opened her box with a frown. "Yeah, I guess you're right, but he's such a great little guy. I wish we could keep him."

Del started eating his dinner. "I don't see how. Solar Drakes are a restricted species. We'll probably get into a lot of trouble if we get caught with him, and not just from the school. Even if you did rescue his egg from Pathal, we should've turned it over to the staff then. And if Pathal tries to get into the room again, we might have a bigger problem. If he triggers more than my alarm, school security could show up and find him." Del sighed. "But, yeah, the drake is such a cute little guy."

Skylar picked up his sandwich. "So what kind of trouble are we talking here? Suspension, a firm talking-to, jail time? I know you've been doing some research on this."

"Unfortunately, it's kinda tricky since so much of the data on Solar Drakes is restricted." Del paused to slurp up a small raw squid. "One thing in our favor is there's no evidence of us ever being in the Armstrong system, so we can't be accused of stealing the egg. If that were the case, we'd be looking at a long-term stay in a prison colony. Beyond that, I can't really tell you what would happen because I can't find evidence of people doing anything more than being arrested for smuggling eggs out of the system. Something about the adults being extremely aggressive in their native habitat. That's one of the reasons Armstrong's Ring is off limits to travelers. There's a small research station there, but that's it."

"Is this that system you had pulled up on your holodisplay the other night?" Skylar set his sandwich back in the box and pulled out some of the fresh carrots. He knew they should be talking about Pathal too, but getting the Solar Drake home would solve all their problems in one fell swoop, if it didn't get them all thrown into a prison colony somewhere.

Del nodded. "That would be it. It's a fairly unique system. The planets that the Solar Drakes come from are actually binary planets in the same orbit around Armstrong. They share an atmosphere, which is really odd, but they're two separate masses. From the little I could find out, the Solar Drakes actually fly in-between the two bodies. What they don't say is *how* the two parts of the planet share an atmosphere. It shouldn't be possible, but it is and there are some very unique species living there."

"I've heard something about those binary planets." Putting her hands over her plate, Solaria defended her meat from the drake as it tried to snatch a piece. "You've already had yours. This is cooked, not raw." She flashed Del a glare at his mistake on her dinner, but he didn't seem to notice.

"This is interesting and all, but it still doesn't help us decide how to handle our problem." Skylar picked up the remainder of his sandwich. "How do we do the right thing by the little guy and not end up getting kicked out of school or worse?"

Solaria sighed. "I've been giving this a bit of thought. Del, is there a stargate at the Armstrong system or close by?"

Del nodded. "There is a gate. If memory serves, it's about eight hours from the Ring."

"Okay." She chewed thoughtfully for a moment. "This might work. I overheard some of the girls saying that there's going to be a trip to the Galaxeria this weekend. There's a lot of traffic in and out of there. The way these trips work is the school ship takes anyone who wants to go, then it's parked there overnight and leaves the next afternoon to come back here." A strange, almost dangerous look crossed her face as she dropped her voice. "If we go on the trip, we could borrow the school ship, get the little guy back to Armstrong's Ring, and then get back to the Galaxeria before anyone knows we aren't there."

Del shook his head emphatically. "You're talking about stealing a space ship. Do you know how much trouble that alone would get us in? Plus, there would be fines for landing on Armstrong's Ring without proper permits."

"And who says we're not going to have the proper permits?" Solaria purred.

A shiver went through Skylar. What she was talking about was dangerous and risky, but they would get the Solar Drake back where it belonged. Wasn't that what was best for the drake? "How do we get the proper permits?"

"Del's the smart one. I'm sure he can think of something." She popped another piece of meat into her mouth. "It shouldn't be too hard to get some permits with all the right information on them to get us in and out of there safely. You've been getting information off the dark web—get this too." Then her eyes sparkled. "We're students. We'll be in a school ship. Couldn't we get some kind of research permit, or a tour of their research facility? You know, the more I think about this, the more I like it."

Skylar nodded. "That sounds a lot more feasible." He glanced at the little drake, still trying to talk Solaria out of more meat. "I just want him somewhere safe, where he can be happy and grow into a proper Solar Drake. Somewhere away from Pathal and the corp-brats."

Del frowned before downing his last squid. "I'm not thrilled with the idea, but you both have valid points. I'll see what I can do about getting something worked out. I've never forged credentials before. I'll have to be careful to make sure they pass security. We'll also need to get our names on the list of kids going to the Galaxeria. If the trip fills up, then we'll have to wait a couple of weeks until the next one. I'm not sure our roommates can be patient that long before they can get peace and quiet again."

Solaria gave in and split the last piece of meat with the little drake. "So, what do you think, little guy? Do you want to go home?"

His big sparkling eyes fixed on Skylar for a moment. A strange feeling passed through him. Then he flew over and landed on Skylar's shoulder and wrapped his tail around Skylar's neck. A soft voice, little more than a whisper of wind, danced in Skylar's mind. *"Home?"*

He stretched himself down Skylar's arm and pulled at the dampening bracelet. It wasn't the first time he'd done that. "Hey, leave that alone." Skylar picked him off his arm and put him on his shoulder. The little guy wrapped his tail back around Skylar's neck and pushed his head against Skylar's ear. The warm happiness that welled up in Skylar told him it was going to be hard to give him up, but it was for the best. He was going to keep telling himself that.

19
Shopping Chaos

SKYLAR MOVED through his exercises, letting his mind be at peace under Professor Aduncus' watchful eye. He was growing accustomed to the professor's mental touch as he monitored Skylar's progress. Although he never told his mentor, he spent at least an hour doing his exercises before each training class so his mind was peaceful and he could hopefully shield any thought of the little drake from Professor Aduncus. The movements were both relaxing and stimulating, and Skylar thoroughly enjoyed them and the opportunity to get the dampening bracelet off. Although he knew that the bracelet was necessary for his own mental health, as well as the safety of those around him, his mind was a lot clearer without the dampener even before he did the exercises.

"You're making a lot of progress, Mr. Mars," Professor Aduncus said from where he sat on the training room floor in a comfortable meditative posture.

"Thank you, sir. You're being most understanding and patient with me."

The professor bowed his bald gray head slowly. *"Once we found a way for you to relax, you've done all the work. You've made all the progressive steps. I'm just a humble guide. I saw your name on the list of the students going to the Galaxeria this weekend."*

Skylar moved to his next stance with a grace he wouldn't have had two weeks earlier. *"That's correct.*

Del and Solaria think it will be good for me to go and do a bit of shopping."

"You'll be faced with an almost surely overwhelming experience. There'll be so many people, so many minds all pushing at you. Not to mention the physical stimulation of the lights, sounds, and people that'll make it hard for you to block things out. It's definitely a good thing that you continue to wear the bracelet. Make sure that nothing happens to it while you're gone. I don't think you're ready to handle an assault on all of your senses. There is no doubt that you will soon, but not just yet."

"I promise that the bracelet won't leave my wrist while I'm gone."

"Very good." Professor Aduncus stood and stretched. *"Now, go and have a good weekend. I'll see you here next week at our regular time. Don't be late."*

Skylar completed the complex movement and then bowed to his mentor. *"Thank you, sir."* He held out his wrist so Aduncus could return the dampening bracelet to its customary place. As the bracelet closed around his arm, the clarity he felt when it was gone vanished in a strange mental haze. Skylar smiled at the professor. "See you next week."

THE TRIP from Stars' End to the Galaxeria was vastly different from the field trip to the museum when they'd saved the egg. On the trip to the museum, most of his fellow students had been fairly restrained, staying in their quiet school personas. Going to the Galaxeria, they were anything but quiet. Skylar was thankful that, for some reason, Pathal and most of his friends didn't appear to be on the ship. It gave him hope they'd be able to get the little drake home without problems. They also got lucky and the bioscanners in the airlock were down, so they didn't detect them taking the drake through.

Del frowned and generally looked unhappy. "I can't believe you guys are dealing so well with everyone being so excited about getting out. I can't hear myself think and I'm just a low-level feeler."

Skylar held up his wrist with the dampening bracelet on it. "I can't feel or read anything right now."

Solaria pulled off her headphones. "What did you just say, Del? I'm trying to block out everything." Like a lot of readers, she used headphones as a way to put some distance between herself and the external stimulus that pounded against her.

"Exactly." Del sighed. "I wish I'd thought to bring my headphones."

"Maybe you can find some at the Galaxeria before we take off," Skylar suggested. He opened his pack but kept it in his lap, below the level of the desk, so he could reach in and pet the fledgling that playfully licked and nipped at his fingers. The movement helped him relax. He'd caught himself stroking and touching the little Solar Drake a lot since they'd made the decision to return it to Armstrong's Ring. A huge part of him didn't want to let the little guy go, even though he knew it was for the best. Since he'd lost his mother, the little drake was the closest thing he had to family. He wondered, more than once, if he might be able to arrange some way to come back and visit, but with the security around the Armstrong system being so tight, that probably wasn't going to happen easily.

Del huffed. "Like I could afford much at the Galaxeria. It may be the biggest shopping station in the galaxy, but it's also one of the most expensive. I heard there are jewelry stores there that have things that cost more than the whole worth of some backwater planets." He glanced at Skylar. "No offense to those that come from backwater worlds."

"None taken." Skylar kept petting the drake. "So, we all remember the plan?"

Both Solaria and Del nodded. "How could we forget the plan?" Solaria asked. "As long as Del remembered all his files and documents"—she air-quoted—"everything should go just fine. The only difficulty I see is trying to find out where to leave the fledgling. I want to make sure the little guy has the best possible chance of survival."

Skylar frowned as something that they hadn't thought of crossed his mind. "We're not going to have time to teach him to hunt. He likes meat. If he doesn't know how to hunt, won't he starve?"

Solaria stopped fidgeting with her headphones for a moment and looked thoughtful. "He's a predator, a very intelligent predator. I bet he can figure it out. Maybe we can leave some meat with him so he's got something to keep him going. We can pick up just about anything at the Galaxeria."

"You know, it might be better if we left him with the researchers," Del suggested. "I figure they can train him to hunt and make sure he survives. He might not even be the first stolen egg to be returned to them. It might happen all the time. They might even have a class set up for little Solar Drakes to learn the skills it takes to survive in their native habitat."

"But then we'll be right back where we are now if we get discovered with him," Skylar added. "We'll get in trouble for having him. The whole reason we came up with this elaborate plan to return him was so we *didn't* get into trouble." He didn't add that the idea of leaving the fledgling with someone else just didn't sit well. He knew that once the little guy was out of their care, there wasn't much he could do to make sure he had a good life, but he wanted to give it his best shot. Anything else felt like a betrayal of hatching him in the first place.

"Why don't we see how the researchers react when we arrive?" Del said. "We'll take the tour of their facility as students and prospective researchers like we planned. If they seem nice enough, then we'll see about leaving his training to them. The tour is how I planned on getting us legally on-world anyway. It was the easiest option to acquire landing clearance."

The Solar Drake nipped at Skylar's fingers. It was a soft, gentle nip and sent a comforting feeling through him. "We'll see. But if it looks like we'll get in more trouble doing that, we'll just fly off to another part of the planet and find a spot with lots of bugs and small creatures for him to eat. Solaria's right. He's a predator; he'll figure out hunting fairly quickly." *If he's even old enough to hunt on his own,* Skylar thought. There was so much about drakes they hadn't been able to find out.

Solaria settled her headphones back on her ears. "Exactly."

Del shook his head as she closed her eyes before turning to address Skylar. "I thought you might like to know, in the middle of planning for this, that I couldn't find anything on the com you got. Whoever sent it to you made sure that it was scrubbed before it was shipped. Sorry."

Skylar shrugged. "Hey, you tried. I'd love to know who sent it and why, but I guess that's something that'll keep for now." With everything going on, he wasn't really worried about who had sent the box or the money. Making sure the Solar Drake was safe was Skylar's primary goal. He'd think about other things later when everything calmed down.

"There's just too much we don't know. I hate not knowing things."

"I'm with you." Skylar smiled at Del. "Tell you what. We've got to promise that when we have kids of our own, we're not going to keep things from them."

Del slumped in his seat and put his head on the desk. "I don't even know if I'm going to have kids. Tursiops still practice selected breeding. My people are very practical when it comes to mates. I'm such a low-level feeler—odds are that my intelligence won't be taken into consideration when I get old enough to begin thinking about mating. Not to mention I haven't gotten the whole idea of what kind of mate I want sorted out."

"Approaching stargate," the pilot announced before Skylar could respond.

"We're almost there." Suddenly, the excitement of their escapade surged, and pushed everything else out of his mind. The slow trip from the academy to the stargate had almost nullified it, but being only a few minutes from the huge shopping station meant that it wouldn't be long before they were commandeering the school ship to get to the Armstrong system. And once they were there, pretty soon the little Solar Drake would be free on his native world. Skylar's throat tightened, and he wasn't exactly sure why.

THE LIGHTS, smells, and sounds of the Galaxeria hit Skylar like a brick thrown against his head. He stood in the hallway that led from the ship's airlock and stared at the magnitude of it all. On the approach, he'd seen the giant space station that floated just beyond the stargate. From what he could tell, they could have easily put six or seven stations the size of Stars' End inside the Galaxeria and still had extra room.

Inside the station, it was even more overwhelming. Every store must have had a bright neon holo-sign that flashed endless advertisements while customers talked and shouted in loud voices.

"Don't block the hall, noob!" Pathal and his cronies shoved past Skylar, Del, and Solaria.

Skylar wondered where they'd been during the trip. He hadn't seen them get on the ship, and although there were several compartments to the school ship and they hadn't gone exploring, he'd just assumed Pathal and crew had stayed back at school. Having him at the Galaxeria made Skylar nervous. The sooner they checked into the Galaxeria rooms they'd reserved for the night, found Del headphones and got back to the ship to leave the airlock, the better he'd feel.

Solaria flexed her claws. "You know, I really could just shred that little corp-brat. We still haven't gotten back at him for trying to break into your room and steal the drake."

Skylar patted her arm. "I think we all could shred him. Why don't we go check into our room? I think you guys said that was the first priority."

Del nodded. "Exactly. Being checked in will help us cover not being here. The rooms we normally get are just around the corner. Once we check in, the chaperones won't worry about us until tomorrow afternoon when we're supposed to report in."

"Won't they think it's odd that we don't have any luggage?" The only time Skylar had been to a hotel back on Hummassa had been when he and his mother were on vacation, and they always had a bag or two with them.

"They probably won't." Solaria turned them down the next hall. "We're with the school. We're here for shopping. Kids always leave with more bags than they came with."

Skylar wished they had the pack that the fledgling was in—it would at least make him feel more legit—but they'd left it on the ship. If they had to get a security person to let them back onto the ship, it was their excuse for being there. Since they were in the school's computers, the ship should let them back on without question. Del figured it would.

After they checked in and had their key cards to their two rooms, they headed into the chaos of the main body of the Galaxeria.

"Should we try and find you some headphones, Del?" Skylar asked.

"Sure, why not?" Del didn't sound overly excited about shopping.

There were even more species in the Galaxeria than there were at Stars' End. Skylar wasn't surprised that he didn't recognize all of them. Sentient beings of every shape, skin color, skin type, and atmosphere walked, flew, floated, or danced through the large galleries that separated the shops. Even out in the galleries, vendors had small carts where they hocked their goods.

Skylar had to sidestep to avoid a short creature with bright green skin wearing a dark suit accented by tiny pale stripes. In doing so, he bumped into a large Tursiops man who was completely bald like Professor Aduncus, but instead of gray skin, his skin was black and white.

"Watch where you're going, human!" roared the man.

Del grabbed Skylar's hand and pulled him away. "We're really sorry, sir. My friend is new here."

Skylar shook his head and followed Del into an electronics store. Solaria already stood just inside the door. "Wow, he was huge and not at all as friendly as the Tursiops at school."

"That wasn't just any Tursiops," Del explained. "That was a member of the Orcan clan. They are the single most dangerous clan on Tursiops. They came close to taking over the planet years ago, until the rest of our people rose up and put them down. On Tursipia, they don't cause trouble anymore, but off world, there are rumors they control a good bit of the black market. Not folks you want to get on the bad side of."

"So, even your peaceful people have their trouble makers?" Solaria asked, falling into step with them. "That's nice to know. There might be hope for you yet, Del."

Del didn't respond. His gaze traveled the store, then he headed to a rack of headphones that looked like they would fit almost every race.

As Del picked out a pair, Skylar looked at Solaria, who looked like she was on guard for something. The only thing missing was her short white and gray fur standing on end. "What's up?"

She shrugged. "Not sure. There's something in the air."

He had no idea what she was talking about, and changed the subject. "Why don't you two just use the dermal coms for music?"

"Since the coms' nanobots communicate directly with our auditory nerves, they don't actually muffle outside noise as they do it. The headphones help block background sounds while they play music or com conversations. We use them more for the blocking than the sounds."

Shouting erupted out in the galley.

"Something's going on." Solaria started for the door. "Come on, let's see what it is."

Skylar looked at Del, still trying to make a decision. "We're going out to see what the excitement's about." He turned and hurried to catch up to Solaria.

In the gallery, the Orcan from before was shouting at someone who looked like a giant pig, complete with white tusks and strange pointed ears, dressed in thick leather. The pig guy had a large cane that he swung at the Orcan. The Orcan caught the cane in a huge webbed hand and yanked it away from the pig.

A high, shrill whistle came from the pig guy.

"The Boarisk is calling for help," Solaria said as they stopped a few feet outside the electronics shop.

"That's a Boarisk?" Skylar asked, staring at the pig. The pictures he'd found online while investigating their movements and habits hadn't done them justice. "They're the ones who attacked Hummassa and killed my mother." Hot rage built up in him. For a moment, he thought about yanking off the dampening bracelet and projecting all the fear and sadness he'd felt that night at the Boarisk.

Then he realized the chaos he could cause as his anger swept through the crowded shopping station. Everyone would know members of the school were there, and they'd all get in trouble. It would probably screw up their mission to get the Solar Drake home.

Solaria put a hand on his arm. "We have to stay out of this. Let the Orcan deal with him. He can wipe the floor with the Boarisk."

True to her words, the Orcan punched the Boarisk hard enough that the tusks protruding from its lower lip shattered as it went down on the purple and blue wood-grained floor, and lay there writhing. Several more Boarisk pushed their way through the crowd.

"Unless you want what he got, you'll take him and go," roared the Orcan.

The Boarisks grabbed their fallen friend, tusks and all, and disappeared into the crowd. Seeing them retreat from something gave Skylar hope that eventually he'd have his revenge against them too.

"Well, that could've been scary," Del said from behind them.

Solaria turned. "That was probably the most excitement we'll see all day. Did you find some headphones? We need to get going."

A security bot appeared and scanned about for the source of the disturbance. The Orcan and Boarisks had already disappeared into the crowd. The security bot rolled over to where the Orcan had dropped the Boarisk cane. It picked it up, carried it over to a trash receptacle, and deposited it.

Skylar stood there for a second. "Wait a minute." He waited until the security bot was several doors down and hurried over to the receptacle. The head of the cane was still sticking up above the other trash there. Skylar removed it.

"Why do you want that thing?" Del asked.

Skylar looked at the ornate silver hog's head that formed the cane's top. There were tiny red stones set for the eyes.

"You're taking it as a trophy aren't you?" Solaria piped in. "Sorta like counting coup. Not bad Skylar. We're going to make a predator out of you yet." She graced him with a huge grin.

He grabbed a piece of paper out of the trash receptacle and wiped off some of the other garbage that stuck to the cane's shaft. "I guess. I don't know. They took everything from me. I might as well have something of theirs. Now let's get out of here before something else happens."

"What's counting coup?" Del asked as they took off through the crowd.

"Taking something special from an enemy when they aren't looking. It's something you can wave around in their faces later," Solaria explained.

Skylar glanced at the cane in his hand. He would definitely like to wave it around in some Boarisk faces later. It felt like he was taking the first steps in taking from them what they had taken from him.

They hurried through the crowd, heading back toward the school ship. Skylar's heart pounded. He couldn't tell if it was from what they'd just seen or what they were about to do. Either way, he knew his life was changing. Again. He just hoped this was the right change.

He'd never forgive himself if something happened to the Solar Drake after they returned it to the wild, or if Del and Solaria got into trouble because of what they were about to do.

20
To Armstrong's Ring

HOPING NO one could hear his nervous thoughts, Skylar peered around the last corner before they reached the airlock for the school ship. Solaria was already there with her hand pressed to the biopad that would either grant them access or keep them locked out. A green light flashed above the pad. She nodded and gestured for Skylar and Del to follow her onto the ship.

Skylar still couldn't believe they were actually stealing the school ship. He didn't doubt they would get into a lot of trouble if they got caught, no matter how good their intentions were, but it would be worth it to make sure the Solar Drake got home safe.

As they passed through the airlock, Del stopped and tinkered with the biopad. After a moment, he stepped past the heavy airlock doors and they slid shut behind him. "That should make it look like there's just a biopad problem if someone tries to get back on the ship before we return."

"And you really think no one's going to try and get back on the ship before tomorrow afternoon?" Skylar asked as they closed the airlock door on the ship side.

"Come on, you've been in school with these kids for almost two months now. Do you really think they're going to want to go back to the academy so soon?" Del started up the metal stairwell that would take them to the upper level of the ship and the flight deck. "This ship never leaves for the academy on time, because the driver and any chaperones normally have to spend hours rounding up students. We'll be fine. While you're warming up the engines, I'll upload a fake signature into the station's computers to make it look like the ship is still docked here. Since there're no windows on this part of the station, they'd have to send a maintenance crew out on an exterior walk to actually notice we're gone."

"Or an arriving or departing ship could spot the empty bay." Skylar opened the flight deck door. There were more than a few holes in their plan, and he just hoped none of them became real problems.

"And how would they know we're supposed to be here?" Del asked as he hurried into the right seat. He frowned as he settled down. "These controls look a bit more complicated than the holofile I found. So far, it's not responding to me. This might take a few minutes"

Skylar sat in the left chair. A rush of adrenaline surged through him. He was actually sitting in a pilot's chair. He was about to fly a starship. It's something he most likely never would've done if he stayed on Hummassa. Something good was finally coming out of the Boarisk attack on his home. His world had expanded, and with any luck, they weren't about to throw it down the drain.

Skylar pushed the negative thoughts aside and tried to focus on what they were doing. Del had calculated the odds of their success—they weren't huge, but not horrible either. So much of their worlds were automated, there was a good chance they might slip out and make it back in one piece without being missed. If everything worked out perfectly. "These controls look a lot like what were on Phil's ship." He touched the steering yoke.

"Scan accepted," an automated voice announced.

"That was quick, Del," Skylar said. He grinned and gripped the yoke. Things were off to a smooth start.

Del glanced at him and shook his head. "That wasn't me. That was the ship's automated scan. I didn't have time to put in the information to get the ship to accept us. It's still fighting me. Somehow you're already in the system. That doesn't make sense." He frowned. "Now it's letting me in"

"Wait a minute, so if we're already registered with this ship, then we're not technically stealing it. Right?" Skylar's hopes for getting out without landing in a huge amount of trouble rose.

"No." Del shook his head. "We're definitely still technically stealing it. Um, let's not use *that* word… we're commandeering it for a vital mission. Yeah, that sounds so much better. I'll worry about why you're already in the system later. Right now, it just makes my job easier. Let's get going."

Del danced his fingers across his tablet and began explaining to Skylar how to get the engines started so they could disconnect from the Galaxeria. The flapping of leathery wings heralded the arrival of the little Solar Drake, Solaria not far behind. The little drake landed on Skylar's left shoulder as he tapped the last button of their pre-launch preparations.

"Stars' End beta, this is Galaxeria control." A stern male voice came over the ship's com. "You are not scheduled for departure until tomorrow afternoon. Please explain why you have started your engines."

Skylar glared at Del. "I thought you had this handled," he hissed, hoping his voice didn't carry to Galaxeria control.

Del's face darkened. "I forgot about their control. It's not like I've spent a lot of time flying on flight decks."

"So, what do we say?" Skylar struggled to keep his voice low.

"Sorry," Solaria said at a normal volume. "We have a special-needs student who has fallen ill and needs to return to the academy before the others are ready. We're just doing a quick run there and will be back in time to pick up the other students tomorrow afternoon. Everything's in order."

Skylar was amazed at how official she sounded.

"We'll adjust your flight plans then," Galaxeria control replied. "Next time, remember to update us before you start your engines. You're clear for departure in three minutes. Galaxeria control, out."

Skylar let out the breath he'd held. "I can't believe we forgot about their control. Of course, they're going to have a control system in place. Wait a minute, why did they buy your story?"

"Because I transmitted the proper access code while she was talking," Del said. "It clicked with me that there should be an access code for the ship, something to identify that we had a right to use it. Since there are multiple teachers and staff who might be piloting it, I figured it would be here somewhere." He pointed to a large label on the top of one of the control panels. "It's right there. If anyone asks us for ID, we transmit that code; it matches the ship's automated code it's always broadcasting. If those codes don't match, they could shut us down and arrest us for stealing the ship."

"Stars' End Beta, you're cleared for departure," said Galaxeria control.

"Here we go then." Skylar hit the button that would disconnect the ship from the airlock. From their window above the airlock, he watched the umbilical retract to the space station, then he pulled back on the yoke to slowly move the ship away from the docking portal.

"I'll get the codes for the Armstrong system fed to the stargate," Del said. "We should be close enough to the gate in a couple of minutes."

"Well, our first step is going smoothly," Solaria said.

Skylar looked over his shoulder at her leaning against the doorframe at the back of the room. "Don't say that. Please don't say that. Every time someone says anything about things going easy—"

"That's when things get interesting." She grinned mischievously.

He turned away from her and pushed the yoke forward to get the ship to move down below the station and toward the stargate.

"Codes for Armstrong have been accepted," Del announced. "I had to put in our visitation permit number, but it went in just fine."

The stargate caught hold of the ship and started pulling it forward, so Skylar let go of the steering yoke.

"Hey, are you all supposed to be flying the ship?" asked a human girl from behind Solaria. She looked to be just younger than Skylar by a few years, but otherwise had similar brown hair and dark blue eyes to his.

The three of them and the Solar Drake turned and stared at her. Solaria looked almost deadly with her brows drawn together and her lips twitching like she was about to snarl or hiss.

"Who are you?" Skylar asked, a huge knot forming in his stomach as he suddenly felt their plan going sideways.

"Melody Porsche." She stared at Skylar and her eyes widened. "What is that?" She pointed at the Solar Drake on his shoulder.

"Ah…" Skylar was hit by a sudden loss of words.

Solaria stalked toward the girl. "Melody, why are you on the ship as opposed to in the Galaxeria shopping or your hotel room?" Her tone was harsh and demanding, an edge of danger to the sound.

Melody stared at her feet and sighed. "My mother cut my credit limit due to my grades slipping. That's actually why I'm at Stars' End—it's cheaper than the school my sisters go to. I can't afford the hotel fee, but I didn't want to tell my friends, so I'm sleeping on the ship."

"We can do that?" Skylar hadn't been given that option. With the limited funds that Ms. Grissom had given him from the money deposited in his account, he'd barely had enough to pay for the hotel room when he split it with Del.

"Not supposed to," Del said.

Solaria sighed and slumped against the wall. "But what are we going to do with you? And I thought all you corp-brats had tons of cash all the time."

Melody shook her head. "Not when our grades aren't good. We… well, some of us… have strict parents. If—"

"If you aren't up to snuff, you get your money yanked. Yeah, we get it." Skylar wished she wasn't there. They were going to have to convince her to keep her mouth shut while they got to Armstrong's Ring and back. She was not a complication they needed. He hoped she wouldn't hinder them in getting the Solar Drake back home.

The stargate lit up. The light drew Skylar's attention away from Melody. Butterflies danced inside him. Before he'd left Hummassa, he'd never dreamed of going through a real stargate. Then when he'd gone through one with Phil, he knew he wanted to be a pilot. Now he was getting the chance, even if they did just commandeer the ship. If he could just remember everything they'd done in the simulator in recent days, everything would be fine.

Entering the gate's event horizon was even more exciting than it had been when Phil was flying. The little Solar Drake tightened his hold on his shoulder as they left normal space. A tiny thrill of excitement emanated from the fledgling. Skylar still couldn't figure out why he picked up emotions and the occasional thought from it even with the dampening bracelet on his wrist.

Then they were back in normal space.

Armstrong, the sun of the system, was a simple yellow star, much like Sol. The stargate was far enough out for it to appear as a mid-size yellow dot in the distance.

"You are entering restricted space," a booming automated voice filled the flight deck. "Please identify yourself."

"Restricted space?" Melody squealed. "Get back in the stargate! Take us back to the Galaxeria or school."

"I've got this." Del quickly entered a code.

"Authorization accepted," the system replied. "Please proceed to the research station on Ring Two. Follow beacon AS32R3. Any deviation from this path will be met with resistance."

Skylar gulped. He wasn't sure if he wanted to know what the system's idea of resistance was. They hadn't been able to find out if the system's defenses were automated or manual.

"Really, we need to go back," Melody continued to object.

Solaria growled and flexed her hands, making her claws slide in and out slowly. "Look Melody, why don't you go back to the room you're sharing with the other corp-brats and play a game or something until we're done here?"

"Hey, you're Solaria, the Pantherian who scored the most goals in the Z-GBall game last week." Melody's voice sounded weaker, and Skylar remembered how scary a Pantherian could be when they were acting aggressive. "That was really awesome. One of the most exciting games I've seen."

Solaria's shoulder's slumped, and Skylar was fairly sure that if her face hadn't been covered in white and gray fur, she would've been blushing. As it was, the insides of her ears turned a brighter pink than normal. "It was, wasn't it?" Her voice lost the dangerous edge.

"Give me a second and their system won't be a problem," Del muttered as he started punching things into the ship's communication's panel. He frowned several times before he looked up from the control panel in front of him. "Okay, I think I've got it. Until I tell it otherwise, the security system should let us go wherever we want. Just in case we don't like the answers we get from the research station personnel."

"How did you do that?" Melody asked.

"I've studied up on what I need to do to get us out of this mess alive," Del snapped.

"Oh," Melody replied. "None of you told me what that is." She pointed back at the Solar Drake.

"It might be better if you don't know that," Solaria said. "The less you know, the less trouble you'll get in if we get caught, or if you blab about this little adventure when we get back to school."

"What's it worth to you for me to keep quiet?" Melody put her hands on her hips and glared at Solaria.

Solaria flashed her fangs. "You corp-brats are all alike. Always trying to see what you can get out of the rest of us. I should just throw you out of the airlock, and then your parents will think Boarisk slavers grabbed you at the Galaxeria and sold you to someone who didn't think you were worth the price they paid and tossed you out of their ship."

Melody deflated. "You wouldn't do that."

"Wanna bet?" Solaria prowled forward.

"I'm sorry." Melody's bottom lip quivered. "I won't tell. Honest. I'll even give you all my allowance when I get my grades up."

Solaria shook her head. "Money. It always comes down to money with you brats."

The ship bucked and slowed to a stop. Skylar looked at his control panel. Everything appeared to be in order.

"What just happened?" Skylar stared at Del hoping for an answer.

Del frantically adjusted controls on his panel.

"Del, did you do something wrong?" Solaria asked as she leaned over the back of his seat.

"This shouldn't have happened," Del replied. "I just shut down the security scans."

Skylar turned and looked at his friend. "What happened?"

"The automated system that's supposed to fly us down has cut out. I wonder if it's tied to the security system I turned off." Del shrugged. "That does make a little sense. That way if you don't pass security, then you don't get the automated beacon to get you down to the research station safely."

"We should still be able to fly down manually, right?" Skylar tried the yoke and the ship maneuvered like it had when they were leaving the Galaxeria. "I think I can do this. If you can get me a path to fly."

"Wait a minute!" Del sounded more than a little nervous. "You want me to plot a course to fly? But navigation's my worst subject. I could fly us into the sun or too close to an asteroid."

Solaria sighed and leaned back against the wall. "Del, what is spatial navigation? It's just using math to figure out where we're going."

"But there's so much to it," he objected. "There're gravity wells, and asteroids-"

"And an angry Pantherian if you don't get it worked out," she cut him off. "Look, you're the smartest kid in the academy. This shouldn't be that hard for you. We know where the planet is. We know where we are. You just draw a line from here to there, bypassing any really large celestial bodies along the way."

"I could help," Melody pipped in. "I'm pretty good with spatial navigation. Where are we?"

"The Armstrong System." Skylar hadn't thought she might prove to be useful. Most of the corp-brats he knew weren't good for anything but making his life worse.

"Did you forget that the Ring is a binary planet?" Del continued as if Skylar and Melody weren't talking. "We're not even sure which one the research station is on. Not to mention that landing on a binary planet is one of the hardest things to navigate through, and this is Skylar's first time flying."

"Binary planet?" Melody asked. "You mean more than just a planet with moons? Like two parts of a planet in close orbit?"

"Yes, that's what they mean," Solaria said.

Not wanting to feel like Del was insulting his flying skills, Skylar straightened up in his seat. "It might be my first time flying, but I've done great in the simulators and I was one of the best players in Galaxy Explorer." He tried to sound more sure of himself than he really was. He needed to give Del the confidence to get them to the Ring and find a safe course down. "You find us a path and I'll make sure we stay on it." The little Solar Drake chirped as if in agreement. "Come on, Del, you're the brains here, you can do this. Besides, if the guys at the research station realize we made it down without a beacon, don't you think that's really going to impress them?"

Del swallowed hard. "Okay. I'll get something worked out. We're lucky that this system doesn't have a ton of planets. Now just hold us steady right here while I get the calculations done. It might take a few minutes."

"Let me see if I can help." Melody pushed past Solaria. She peered at the screen Del was looking at. "This is an interesting system. I wonder why it's restricted." She fell into easy conversation with Del as they worked together to get the course laid in and told Skylar how to navigate through the system, avoiding the planets, moons, and asteroids that popped up in their path.

ARMSTRONG'S RING came into view. At first, it just looked like an odd-shaped green planet, more egg-like than round, surrounded by the stellar dust cloud rings that gave the system its name. But as they drew closer, it became obvious that there were two large bodies, each about twice the size of a standard moon, with only a short distance separating them.

"Okay, I think I've got a signal from the research station," Del announced. "Let me make a few adjustments to our course. They're on the far side of the starboard planetoid."

"I've never seen anything like it." Solaria peered over the back of Skylar's seat while petting the Solar Drake perched there. "I don't know if I like all the green or not. It's nothing like Pantheria. It also looks really hot."

"It's really pretty," Melody added. "I bet even my mom has never seen anything like this."

Del nodded. "It is hot. It's on the high end of standard habitability." He glanced over his shoulder at Solaria. "You might have problems with the temps."

An updated course appeared on Skylar's control panel. He turned the yoke slightly to allow for the correction. "How long until we land?"

"With proper braking and if we've got the angle of descent right, and if the gravity from the left planetoid doesn't interfere, we should be on the ground in about ten minutes."

"Nine minutes thirty-seven seconds," Melody said, sounding more exact than Del. It felt odd for someone to be more on pinpoint than Del who had a tendency to get the fact dead on.

Skylar nodded. "Good, 'cause I've really got to pee." He got out of his seat and hurried to the crew lavatory.

AS THEY cleared the dust cloud and entered the atmosphere, the ship bucked roughly and Skylar had to grip the yoke firmly to keep them on the course Del set. He struggled as the ship pulled hard to the right. A light flare started on the ship's nose. The light made it difficult for Skylar to see where they were going and he really hoped they weren't about to crash. It was his first landing and the school ship was on the large side for atmospheric maneuvering. As they started down he was thankful they weren't in the same ship they'd taken to the museum, they'd have had to us a shuttle to get down.

"We're about to be on instruments only for forty-three seconds," Del said.

The light flare intensified and a security shield dropped into place over the window as Skylar blinked spots out of his eyes. He focused on the control panel in front of him, displaying a bright yellow line indicating the path they were following with a blue ship-shaped icon. The strain of holding the yoke on their course caused an ache in his arms, but he didn't say anything as the ship continued to buck through the atmospheric turbulence.

The blast shield rose to reveal a thick jungle canopy rushing toward them.

"You might want to pull up a bit, Skylar," Solaria said.

"Yeah, we don't need to crash!" Del wasn't as calm as Solaria.

"Crashing would be bad!" Melody added as she clung to the back of Del's chair.

Skylar pulled back on the yoke and the ship's nose lifted as they leveled out. They skimmed over the canopy, only missing the tallest trees by twenty feet or so.

"The research station should be coming into view about now," Del announced.

They cleared the trees and instantly spotted a series of small buildings sitting along the edge of a large valley. There were three other ships parked near the buildings.

"Looks like the far side of the ships is our best bet." Solaria pointed past the other vessels.

There weren't any people obviously moving around. Skylar fired the landing thrusters like he'd done in the simulator and they slowed even more. It took him several flybys to get close to lined up with the others. Then he slowly brought it down. Even with the instruments, he couldn't judge exactly how close they were to the ground when he cut the landing thrusters. The ship dropped about ten feet before it hit the green grass. The landing jarred all of them, throwing Skylar and Del against their control panels while Solaria and Melody hit the floor hard. Only the fledgling stayed where it was, clinging tight to the back of the pilot's chair.

"Okay, I guess any landing you can walk away from is a good one." Solaria stood and dusted herself off. "But, Skylar, I, for one, think you need a bit more time in the simulator before you try landing on a planet again, at least, if we know it's going to be an unassisted landing."

Skylar nodded and rubbed his head. His hair was slick with sweat and it was running down his forehead toward his eyes. "I agree. But hey, we're here."

"Yeah, we've arrived." Del sat up and twisted in his seat. "It feels like everything's fine. Let's go see what's going on at the research facility. The sooner we get back to the Galaxeria, the less chance we've got of getting into deep trouble."

"Not horrible for a first landing," Melody said. "My dad said he was the only person he knew of who didn't crash a ship the first couple of times they tried."

Her words didn't help him much, but he pushed them out of his mind. "Okay." A knot formed in Skylar's stomach as he looked back at the drake on the pilot's chair. He didn't really want to say goodbye to the little guy. He rubbed his small yellow head. "You stay here for now, okay? We'll be back when we figure out what's going on. Then we'll make sure you get a good home."

The little drake caught Skylar's finger in his mouth and held it softly. *"Home."*

Skylar swallowed hard, then stood and followed Del, Melody, and Solaria out and down the stairs that would lead to the hatch to let them out of the ship.

21
Searching For The Researchers

THE AIR outside the ship was thick and hot. It felt like walking into a wall of water and took Skylar's breath away. "Are you sure we can breathe this stuff?" he gasped.

Del nodded. "Yeah, it's a ninety-eight percent Sol Three-level atmosphere and the other two percent are not dangerous gasses for humans and human-like life forms. I did what research I could before we left. If we'd needed them, I'd have gotten us breathers."

Solaria grabbed hold of the hatch for support. She drooped and the skin around her eyes looked pale.

Skylar stopped and stared at her. "Solaria, what's wrong?" He hoped they weren't killing her with their adventure onto the strange planet.

"The temperature and humidity are too much for me." She paused to pant for a second. "I'll need to grab an envirosuit before I can go out there. We Pantherians aren't made for hot environments. You three go on, I'll catch up. I guess there's some advantages to being human and aquatic."

"We can wait," Skylar offered. He didn't like the idea of splitting up. In stories and videos, that was always when something bad happened.

"No, go on," Solaria insisted. "They probably saw us land. If we take too long, they'll come looking for us. I'll be along in a couple of minutes. If the suits aren't in the closet up here, they'll be in the back of the ship."

"Okay." Skylar looked at Del and Melody, who were already halfway to the nearest building. "We'll see you in a few minutes. If you take too long, we'll come find you." He hurried after them.

"I was wondering about that," Del said as Skylar caught up.

"About what?" Skylar and Melody said in unison.

"About whether or not she was going to need a suit here." He shook his head. "Solaria can be very stubborn. I figured she'd try to move around here unencumbered, just to save face. It's a good thing she went back for the suit. She'll feel a lot better. Plus, I don't want to have to carry her back to the ship after she passed out from the heat."

Skylar held up his hand for Del to be quiet. His gut was still knotted from worry about what was going to happen to them and the Solar Drake. He hoped he didn't come across as rude, but he really wanted Del to not run on like he was prone to do. "I get it. So, any idea which of these buildings we need to look in to find the research team?" He didn't bother to add that he already had a steady stream of fresh sweat trickling down his back, and the heavy, sweet smell of rotting vegetation was getting to him.

"They didn't say in the communication I received accepting my request to come for a tour. Let's just start at the first one."

The buildings were low and made of simple adobe. They reminded Skylar of structures back on Hummassa. These seemed to have a lot more windows, but with the higher temperatures, that was probably needed. The door to the first building was primitive, rough-cut wood. Del pushed it open. Beyond the door looked like a reception area, with a single metal desk and some mismatched chairs. There wasn't anyone there.

"Hello!" Skylar called out, hoping they would get an answer.

They waited, but no one called back.

"It's light outside. I doubt they're asleep," Del said. "Unless this is one of those groups who believe in afternoon naps."

"I don't even know how day and night work on a binary planet," Skylar said as he stared at some of the pictures on the walls. Most of them were of Solar Drakes like their fledgling. There seemed to be a wide variety of colors to the little flying lizards, but none of them looked like they grew very big. Even the larger ones looked friendly, in a reptilian sort of way.

Del didn't respond immediately. "You know, that's something I forgot to look up before we set out. There aren't that many binary planets like this in the galaxy, so there's not a lot recorded about them."

"I'd never heard of them before," Melody said, peering at the pictures of the Solar Drakes. "Is this why we came here—you're bringing him back to his home?"

Skylar nodded in response to her, then answered Del. "Maybe you can ask the researchers if we ever find them. Hello! Is there anyone here?" he called out again.

"Do you think we should try one of the other buildings?" Del asked. "With the other ships parked out there, I would expect there to be someone here."

Skylar nodded. "Me too. Yeah, let's go check the next building. Did you have a time for our tour?"

Del shook his head. "I told them I wasn't completely sure when we'd be arriving. They said just stop in when we got here. It sounded like they're fairly loose with their schedules."

"You guys had this all really planned out, didn't you?" Melody asked as she turned away from the pictures.

"I like planning things out," Del replied, a little shorter than he normally would. It made Skylar wonder if the two of them had had a conflict at school, or if Del was just irritated because she'd helped him with the navigation. It had ended up being a little more complicated than either one of them could figure out on their own. Even though he never would've thought to say it about a corp-brat, he was happy she was along with them.

Skylar tested the single door behind the metal desk. It was locked. He knocked on it. After several minutes, there was still no answer. "Okay, let's keep trying buildings. Maybe they all went to eat at the same time."

On their way, Skylar glanced around to see if Solaria was heading toward them, but didn't spot any sign of her either. He hoped she wasn't having trouble getting into her suit.

The second building looked just like the first from the outside, but the door led to a hallway with several more doors. They stopped just inside the door. "Hello!" Skylar called out again.

This time he didn't wait very long before going to the first door. It was unlocked. Inside looked a lot like a medical office, but everything appeared designed for smaller-than-human patients. There wasn't anyone or anything in it. Even the computer terminal was turned off.

As they worked their way through the building, there were more rooms like the first and the last two doors opened into a storeroom and a small office.

"At least this computer is on," Del said, glancing at the desk that was the twin of the one in the reception room. "The screensaver is on, so it's been deserted for a while, but the power saver mode hasn't kicked in. We know that someone's been here recently."

"I wonder why their tech is so old." Melody looked at the computer. "Some of this stuff is older than we have at school. I bet they don't get a ton of funding."

It was something Skylar hadn't really noticed, since it was all similar to what he was used to back on Hummassa, but he nodded as he looked at more pictures on the wall. There was also a pair of large maps that almost had to be the Ring. There were several spots marked with various colored dots on both planetoids. "I wish we'd brought a tablet along. Having these maps might help us find a good place to release the fledgling."

"Use your dermal com," Del said.

Skylar looked at the metal square on the inside of his wrist. "What? These things can take pictures?"

Del walked over to him. "Yeah, didn't anyone bother to instruct you in the use of your com? They're for more than just keeping in touch." He held the hand with his com on it up to the maps one at a time and tapped it before going on to the second map. "There, I've got it. Let's hope we don't need it."

"I guess we try the next building." Skylar sighed. "I wonder if we should go check on Solaria. She's taking an awfully long time. How long does it take to put on an envirosuit?"

"We can check the reception area and see if she's waiting for us there." Del marched out the door and Skylar followed.

He was beginning to get the feeling that there was something wrong at the research facility.

When they got outside, Skylar resisted laughing. Solaria waddled awkwardly in the envirosuit. It looked like she couldn't get her limbs to move right as she lumbered toward them.

"You know, I really don't like this miserable place," she grumbled as she got close. Her whiskers brushed the clear face shield as she talked. "How you three can stand the heat is beyond me, but this suit is almost worse. It's cool, but it's not flexible at all. How do they use these things to do space walks and hope to have any flexibility?"

Del laughed. "You've got it on backward. I don't see how you managed to get the helmet on with the suit in that position."

The dark glare Solaria threw him was almost enough to melt the protective face shield. "That explains why I broke two helmets trying to get one in place. I don't suppose the buildings are cool enough for me to turn this thing around so I can move easier?"

Skylar shook his head. He managed to not smile at her situation and further enrage her. "Nope, about as warm in them as it is out here."

"I'll go back to the ship. Have you guys found anyone yet?"

"No," Del said without any mirth. "We're still looking. We've been through the first two buildings and nothing."

"I'll hurry." Her frown deepened before she turned away from them to return to the ship. "Something feels not right here. After we check the other buildings, we'll try checking the ships."

"I'll go with you," Melody said, falling into step with Solaria as they headed to the ship. "It'll go faster with two sets of hands."

AN HOUR later, after thoroughly searching all the buildings and being unable to investigate any of the ships without giving Del time to try to crack their security, they still hadn't found any people in the research facility.

"Hey guys," Solaria called as they circled the back of the buildings. "We might want to go this way. It looks like a large number of people went over this grass within the past couple of hours."

Skylar stared at the flattened grass trail leading from the buildings into the jungle that surrounded the small valley. "How can you tell it was in the past couple of hours? This path could've been here for years."

She shook her head. "Predators track things. I've been following trails for years." She knelt down and picked up a broken piece of grass. "See how the broken section is still damp? This didn't happen that long ago. I'd say shortly before we landed."

"You think they ran away because we were coming?" Skylar looked from the trampled grass to the jungle, then glanced at Del. "You don't think there was something wrong with either your communications with them or in your breaking of their system security? Maybe they noticed the beacon is down and went to hide in the jungle until we're gone."

Del shook his head. "There wasn't anything wrong in my communications with them. They might've realized there was a problem with their security." He glanced at Solaria. "You can't smell anything through that helmet, can you?"

She glared at him. "I got a big enough whiff of the jungle from the ship's hatch. I don't really want to smell much more of this place."

"Do you think you could handle taking the helmet off for a minute or so to get a smell of the trail here?" Del gestured to the trampled grass.

"Why would I want to do that?"

"To get a scent of the people who walked this way. See if you can at least tell what species they are."

Skylar looked back at the ships parked in the meadow. "Or could you look up the registration markings of those ships?" He looked at Del.

Del slumped slightly. "I didn't even think of that. It would at least tell us their planet of origin. But how will that help us find the researchers?"

"It might not, but I agree with Solaria—there's something not right here. Knowing where those ships came from might help us figure out something." The feeling of wrongness intensified in Skylar. It was beginning to feel like his scalp was on fire with it.

"Let's go back to the ship and see what we can figure out." Del headed back toward Stars' End Beta at a fast clip. Melody followed him, and it sounded like she was offering help to look up information.

Solaria walked along at a slower pace with Skylar. "I think you might be right. But we don't need to waste time here. I was hoping we'd be back in space by now and heading toward the stargate."

"I know." Skylar nodded. "But we've got to make sure the fledgling has a good start and to do that, we need to talk to the researchers." He sighed. "I wish Del was a stronger feeler. He might be able to pick up something that would lead us to them."

"And this blasted suit makes me so uncomfortable… I don't know if I could read anyone out here or not, and you've got that dampening bracelet on."

Skylar stopped and stared at the bracelet on his wrist. "Do you think it would be safe for me to take it off? We're in the middle of a jungle on a restricted world. It's not like the Galaxeria. I won't be able to hurt people out here, would I?"

The idea stopped him cold. He was finding a way to use his psychic skills for good. It felt good seeing that some of the things they were being taught actually worked and had real-world applications. It was the first time he'd considered doing something like this. He hoped his mother would have understood. He was quickly learning that the thing she'd hated the most could actually be used for good. More than once, he'd begun to wonder why she'd feared psychics so much. Maybe, if she was still alive, he'd be able to tell her they weren't all bad, but she wasn't and all he could do was hope she would comprehend.

"Wait until Del gets done with his scan," Solaria suggested, walking a few feet ahead of him. "If something went wrong, I'm not sure I could get the bracelet back on you quickly, thanks to this suit. But I think it's worth a try."

Del and Melody disappeared into Stars' End Beta.

Shaking himself out of his thoughts, Skylar hurried to catch up with Solaria before she noticed he'd stopped. "I guess everything was going too smoothly. It was probably too much to think that this would be easy."

Solaria chuckled as he reached her side. "I'd be fine with a bit of adventure if I wasn't in this suit. We *had* to rescue the egg of a flying reptile who lives on a jungle planet and then decide to bring him home."

"Yeah, I guess next time we need to plan our adventure a little better or you need to let the corp-brats just torture the poor unhatched critter." Skylar thought about the differences in Pathal and Melody. Although he was still getting to know Melody, he couldn't see her torturing anything the way Pathal seemed to delight in tormenting things.

She shook her head. "You should know by now that I couldn't do that. It's one thing to kill something in a hunt with the intent to eat it; it's entirely different to cause harm to the helpless, no matter what species it is."

Blaster fire roared in the distance. A flock of creatures flew into the sky with loud raucous cries.

"We might know where the researchers are." Skylar stared in the direction of the sound.

"A hunt." Solaria beamed. "I'm ready for a hunt." Then she frowned and held up her thickly-gloved hands. "But I can't use my claws and I left all my weapons back in my room at the academy."

"You think we should go find out what's going on?" Skylar tried to figure out what to do. They could get back in the ship and go back where they belonged. But that didn't help the fledgling. They'd come here for him, to give him a good life. They had to do what they could to make sure everything turned out okay.

Del came running out of the ship's hatch, with Melody steps after him. "What was that noise?"

The little Solar Drake flew behind them. When it saw Skylar, it soared over and landed on his shoulder. A sense of worry flowed from the little guy.

"Blaster fire to the north," Solaria said, pointing in that direction. "Did you think to bring any weapons?"

Del blinked at her. "Do I look like a guy who carries weapons? The closest thing to a weapon I own is a fishing net that I left back with my parents at home!"

"Maybe there's something in the reception building," Skylar suggested.

"You can't be thinking we need to stay here and get in the middle of something, are you?" Melody said as Skylar turned toward the reception building.

"We've got to see what's going on." Skylar broke into a run. More blaster fire erupted in the jungle.

The reception area was still empty and the back door was still locked. Skylar slammed into it with his shoulder. The wooden door held against him.

"Here, let me try," Solaria said from the doorway. "Let's see if I can give it a little mover push as I hit it."

"Mover push… Del, I almost forgot. We want to get my bracelet off, see if my powers can help us in this." Skylar thrust his wrist toward Del. "Solaria was worried she couldn't get it back on fast enough if something went wrong."

Del frowned. "I want to go on the record right now that I don't like any of this, but we need to find the researchers, and one of the ships out there isn't broadcasting an ID code. Its markings aren't coming up either." He took the bracelet off Skylar and slipped it into his pants pocket. "Let's just be really careful."

Once the bracelet came off, Skylar's mind cleared. The first thing he felt was the little Solar Drake sitting on his shoulder.

"Can you hear me now?" it asked in the same soft voice Skylar had heard bites and pieces from for days.

Skylar blinked at it. *"Yes, I can hear you."*

22
Filzbalm

"LOOK OUT, boys." Solaria charged through the reception room. Without his dampening bracelet on, Skylar saw the glow of power shimmering just off her shoulder. He hadn't seen her using her mover powers without the bracelet on since the day they'd met and she'd been messing with his hair. It was impressive.

The door splintered as she hit it. She stumbled but regained her footing. He knew her well enough to know she'd feel horrible if she'd actually hit the floor.

"That worked. It would've been easier without this suit." She wiped her shoulder, knocking a few splinters off.

"Did either of you two know that Solar Drakes can talk?" Skylar asked as he recovered from the spectacle of her ramming the door.

"They can what?" Del stared at the little guy on Skylar's shoulder. "I didn't hear anything."

"I can hear him in my mind," Skylar explained.

"We really should hurry—the others are very afraid. The strangers are after more eggs." A sense of urgency flowed with the words in Skylar's mind.

"Yeah, there was something about that in the information on the reception desk," Melody said. "I scanned through it while you guys were looking in one of the other rooms."

"Interesting," Del said. "I wonder if that's why they're so attracted to readers. You can hear them and everyone else can't. Makes sense. But there are other telepathic races in the universe, and their systems aren't restricted. There's got to be more to it than just they're telepathic."

"I don't know everything yet, but he says that there are strangers who are after more eggs. I bet the ship that's not broadcasting any signal is a raider of some kind." At the mention of raiders, Skylar flashed back to the Boarisk attack on Hummassa. If the Solar Drakes were under a similar attack, they had to do something to help. He suddenly wondered if the inhuman screaming he'd been hearing in his dreams was Solar Drakes crying out for help.

"Sounds feasible," Solaria said. "Let's check this building for any kind of weapon I can use and we'll go save some Solar Drakes." She turned and hurried down the hall beyond the door.

They searched the building. Overall, it was more equipment and the communications system for the research station, along with computer storage banks. In the back room, they found what they were looking for.

"It's not much," Solaria announced. "I think this is an electron net of some sort. It immobilizes things. These look like stunners. They have a couple of settings, but I don't think they'll kill. I was hoping for something like a crossbow or even a spear or two, but these'll have to do."

Fear and terror washed over Skylar. He grabbed hold of the cabinet they'd found the stunner in to keep his balance. His head throbbed. The emotions he was picking up felt like a hundred people all screaming in terror at the same time.

"Here, let me help." The little drake wrapped his tail around Skylar's neck. At the touch, the emotions faded into the background.

"Are you okay, Skylar?" Del asked, touching his arm.

Skylar nodded. "I am now. A wave of emotions hit me, but he blocked it. He knew how to help me." He stared into the drake's sparkling eyes. It felt like they were looking into each other's souls. It was more intense than any of his training with Professor Aduncus and in a second, he accepted what he'd been avoiding in all the training.

Skylar felt the last dregs of his resistance to his psychic powers fade away. He'd been born with his gifts. It was time he really embraced them. He could find a way to honor his mother's memory that didn't involve continuing to fight who he was. All he would accomplish by denying a huge part of himself would be to create a danger to himself and the universe around him.

"Do you have a name?"

"My kind are always born with a name," he replied. *"But you can call me what you would like best."*

Skylar shook his head. *"No, I'll call you by your name. What is it?"*

"I am Filzbalm."

Del was saying something, but Skylar was so engrossed in his mental conversation that all he could hear was background noise. Del shook him. "Skylar, the fear's getting stronger—even I'm starting to feel it. We need to do something."

The shaking broke Skylar and Filzbalm's locked gaze. Skylar blinked.

"Del's right. We have to do something," Filzbalm said.

"Filzbalm agrees with you." Skylar took one of the stunners Solaria held out to him. "Is this on the highest setting? If they won't kill, I want to make sure we knock the bad guys out good. No one's leaving this planet with more drake eggs." He would do everything he could to protect Filzbalm's people. Although the little drake might not look even as human as Solaria or Del, he was still a living being. Skylar felt bad at thinking of him as a pet for weeks.

She nodded. "Of course, I have them on the highest setting." She handed Del the net. "You said you have a fishing net at home, so you probably know how to use this better than I do." Then she handed him a stun pistol. "And use this when you don't have the net." She also passed a pistol to Melody. "It's fairly easy to use, just point at a target and squeeze the trigger."

Melody looked a little scared, but nodded as she pointed the pistol at the ground.

As they walked outside, Solaria looked at the trail. "They went this way."

Filzbalm launched off Skylar's shoulder at a slightly different angle than the direction the trail led. *"Follow me, I know where they are!"*

"Follow Filzbalm," Skylar said, and the four of them ran after the little yellow drake as it flew toward the jungle and weapon fire.

"Who's Filzbalm?" Solaria shouted after him.

But Skylar didn't answer or wait to see if Solaria and Del followed them or stuck to the trail she'd found. The sense of terror grew, and for a moment, Skylar couldn't tell if it was his or coming from someone else.

23
To The Rescue

THE JUNGLE closed in on them quickly. Skylar kept up with Filzbalm, but Solaria quickly fell behind.

"Skylar!" Del shouted. "She's having trouble keeping up. The suit's slowing her down."

Skylar stopped and glared back at his friend. *"Do you want to let everyone know we're here?"*

Del grabbed his head. "There's no need to be so loud."

"I'm sorry." Skylar hurried back to Del. He hadn't realized he could project so strongly as to cause pain. It reminded him of how much training he still had to undergo. "I didn't mean to be so loud. I don't want to hurt you."

"Your mental voice is more forceful, louder than my grandfather's." Del rubbed his temples. "Try toning it down a bit. I bet they could hear you clear into the next solar system."

"I really am sorry." Worry for Del stabbed through him. "I'm still getting the hang of the telepathy stuff, and I didn't have time to do my centering exercises."

"I'll be okay in a few minutes," Del replied. "Look, you and Melody go on ahead with the fledgling. Solaria and I will catch up. Don't do anything stupid until we get there. Okay? We have to do all the stupid things together."

Skylar smiled and nodded. "Okay. If I need to, I'll send Filzbalm back to you and hope he can help you understand what's happening." He glanced at the Solar Drake, suddenly realizing he hadn't asked if he minded.

"That's fine," Filzbalm replied.

"Thanks." Skylar knew it was going to take a little time to get used to Filzbalm being more like a person and less like a pet.

"So that's his name, huh—Filzbalm." Solaria huffed as she plodded up to them. "Just go on. We'll catch up. I've got to get someone to redesign these suits. They aren't made for ease of terrestrial travel."

"Okay, you two be safe." Skylar hurried toward Filzbalm where the little drake had perched on a low-hanging branch. As he approached, Filzbalm launched into the air and headed deeper into the jungle.

The feeling of terror grew as they traveled further into the dense trees and vines. Skylar pushed at the sensations like Professor Aduncus had shown him. It helped keep the exterior feelings from overwhelming him. Filzbalm's constant presence in his head helped too. The little Solar Drake was more soothing to him than the dampening bracelet had been, and gave him the strength to keep going.

Huffing, but keeping her complaints down, Melody crashed through the jungle behind them. "Keep going, I'm doing fine."

"We're not far now. I can hear the angry cries of a nesting female. I wonder if that's what my mother sounded like when my egg was stolen."

The realization that they were both orphans hit Skylar hard. It gave him even more drive to make sure no other eggs were stolen, and no more hatchlings had to rely on the stumbling guesses of ignorant people to survive their first few weeks. They had gotten lucky, and he hoped they hadn't stunted Filzbalm too much, particularly since he could hear the little guy without his bracelet on and wondered how much more mental attention he had really needed.

Filzbalm landed on a branch again. The noise ahead of them sounded really close. *"Careful, Skylar, we don't want them finding you too soon."*

Skylar stopped behind a tree. Melody slid to a stop right next to him. A high-pitched cry of anger rang above the other noises of the jungle. Another blaster shot boomed. The cry turned to pain.

Skylar gripped the stunner. He didn't have much experience shooting guns other than in games. In Galaxy Explorer, he'd always let Teir do most of the shooting. He'd been the pilot. But he had to do everything he could to help. It was just him, Filzbalm, and Melody in that moment.

He peered around the trunk of the tree and his blood went cold. Three Boarisk holding large weapons stood in the clearing. There were two humans with them, and what he assumed was a Volarian, what with its radiant white skin and vivid red hair. The humans and Volarian looked to be prisoners. Across the small clearing, one of the Boarisk walked over to a huge Solar Drake, five or six times Filzbalm's size, on the ground and kicked it. Skylar's blood ran cold. They were too late to save the mother drake. He gripped his stunner so hard his fingers hurt.

"The female's down." The Boarisk turned to their prisoners. "Now, where is the nest? You know the eggs won't survive without the female anyway. Don't make us find the male and kill it too."

One of the humans, a man with long blond hair and a thick beard, frowned at the Boarisk. "Why are you killing these poor creatures? They have as much right to live as you do."

"More!" the Volarian hissed.

"And you think I don't want these eggs to live?" The Boarisk laughed. It was a harsh sound that reminded Skylar of blaster fire. "They're no good to me dead. The last ones I stole, one of them failed to get to its buyer. My men lost it, but no matter." He swung his blaster from one researcher to another, like he was trying to make up his mind which one to shoot first. "I managed to get on and off this stupid world without alerting you last time. This time it was even easier. Your security system is pathetic, but I don't know where any more nests are. Now, you'll show me where this female's nest is or I'll keep killing your people. The market for Solar Drakes is strong among the corporate readers, and I aim to make them happy."

Skylar glanced at Filzbalm. These were the raiders who stole his egg. Was his mother dead too, like the poor drake on the ground in front of them? He couldn't let them do it again. *"Filzbalm, are there more drakes in the jungle around here? Can they help us?"*

"I will find them." Filzbalm dropped from the branch and took off for the denser jungle.

The stunner in Skylar's hand grew heavier as he turned his gaze back to the clearing. He forced himself to relax his hold on the composite stock. The Volarian glared at the Boarisk and the two appeared locked in a silent battle of wills. Then the Boarisk laughed again.

"Your mind tricks won't work on me." He pointed to his head. "I always make sure to wear a telepathic blocker when I come here. I know that readers and Solar Drakes go hand in hand, and I like to be prepared." He slapped the Volarian, sending her tumbling backward into the thick tangle of bushes. "We Boarisk are mostly immune to you telepaths anyway."

Skylar tightened his grip on the stunner again. He couldn't wait anymore. Glancing at Melody, he mouthed. "Shoot when I do, then get down." He brought his weapon up and fired at the Boarisk, then ducked back behind the massive tree even as the two beams of light shot across the glade.

"What was that?" the Boarisk roared. "Are there more people out there?"

They both missed. Skylar slumped against the tree for a moment. What could they do? Telepathy wouldn't work on him and they were both terrible shots.

What about empathy? How would he and his men react to a feeler attack?

"Hamfield, go find the shooters!"

"I'm going to try something," he whispered to Melody. "Do you have any way to block psychic attacks?"

"I'm just a low-level feeler, lower than Del. I can shield most attacks though." Her brow creased in concentration. "Okay. Hit them hard."

Hoping he wasn't about to hurt her, Skylar took a deep breath. He didn't have time to go through the complex movements he used at school to center his mind. So, he simply remembered the terror he'd felt as he entered the jungle. He recalled the pain, fear, and worry he experienced when the Boarisk raiders attacked Hummassa. He shut his eyes tightly, sunk to his knees and tried desperately not to let the emotions overwhelm him before he could unleash them as he churned them over and over in his mind.

"There's a human boy over here, Captain," a guttural voice called out. "A female too."

Opening his eyes, Skylar lashed out with the emotional weapon he'd formed. A squeal of terror was his reward as the Boarisk who had come within a few steps of him caught the full brunt of his empathic assault. The pig-like creature fell to the ground, grabbed its head in its thick, hoof-like hands, and continued to squeak and scream.

The jungle exploded around him as Solar Drakes of every size and color poured out of the greenery and dove at the Boarisk raiders before Skylar could focus his attack on them. The emotions he used on his attacker surged within him. Too vividly, he remembered his mother's hand sticking out of the broken windshield before the hover car exploded.

The terror of the Solar Drakes and the researchers hammered at him. He pushed it away. It fought him. The emotions struggled in his grasp and tried to overwhelm him. On his hands and knees, he tried to find his center again. He was totally unaware of what was going on around him as he fought to regain control. Shots rang out. Heavy weapons and light. Something squealed in terror. The drakes roared, sounding very large and ferocious, but there was nothing for him to focus on.

Joy surged and mingled with fear. Sadness and sorrow radiated out and engulfed him. The thick dank smell of the jungle engulfed him. It was all too much. He couldn't find a center. He couldn't focus. Everything swept Skylar away as the chaos consumed him. The part of him that was Skylar was lost, pulled away by a river of sensations he couldn't control.

Then a light weight landed on his shoulder, and a warm, scaly tail wrapped around his neck. The emotional storm around him receded. Skylar's breath came in short gasps as he found his center and pushed his own emotions back into the recesses of his mind where they belonged. It was a lot easier without all the external things pounding on him.

"Come back to me, Skylar." Filzbalm's mental voice was soothing. *"It's okay. We're going to be fine. You're going to be fine."*

With shaking fingers, Skylar reached up and stroked Filzbalm's head. "Did we win?"

"This nest is safe."

"And the Boarisks?" Skylar tried to sit up, but his head spun.

"The one who was able ran. The other two are still on the ground."

"And if I have anything to say about it, they'll stay there." The blond man appeared in Skylar's vision. "Thank you for your timely save." He reached out a hand to help Skylar stand. "Are you Del Aduncus?"

As he stood, Skylar shook his head. "No, Skylar Mars. Del's my roommate and good friend. We came here for a tour."

The man frowned at Skylar. "With your powers, you should know better than to lie, even if it was just a bending of the truth." His gaze landed on Skylar's shoulder and Filzbalm. "You came because of this little guy. I think we need to discuss this when we get back to the office. But first, we need to secure these two raiders, then track down their captain."

A strange knot formed in Skylar's stomach. "Okay." They were going to be in trouble. They'd saved the day, but that wasn't going to matter. Everything had just gotten a lot more complicated.

Three massive explosions shook the jungle. More birds and Solar Drakes took to the sky in a cacophony of sound and color.

24
Picking Up The Pieces

SKYLAR, MELODY, and the two other humans ran through the forest to get back to the clearing where a thick column of black smoke rose into the twilight sky. Around them, the Solar Drakes flew like they knew what was happening and wanted to help. It was strange, because they weren't acting as intelligent as Filzbalm did.

"Did you have anyone with you besides the girl?" the blond asked as they raced onward. A brown Solar Drake flew next to his shoulder, easily keeping pace with him.

"Yeah, Del and our friend Solaria," Skylar said. *"They should be around here somewhere."*

"Let's hope that the Boarisk didn't get them on his way back to his ship, and that they didn't get caught in the explosions." The blond jumped an outstretched tree root. *"I'm Doctor Wellengrad, by the way. Thank you for helping my team, or what remains of us."*

Skylar didn't bother to hide his dislike for the species. *"I have personal issues with the Boarisk myself. Anything I can do to upset them is a good thing."* He ducked under a low-hanging branch with large purple fruit on it.

"Skylar!" Del shouted from out of the greenery at the edge of the clearing. "What's going on?"

Skylar skidded to a halt. "Del, is Solaria with you? Are you okay?"

Del nodded as Solaria extracted herself from the underbrush.

"We're fine!" Del shouted. "We tried to follow the running Boarisk guy, but the explosions knocked us back here."

"I really don't like this suit," Solaria growled. "I could've caught him if I hadn't been in it. You know, maybe I hate this stupid little planetoid too. If it wasn't so hot here, I wouldn't be like this."

Doctor Wellengrad stopped and stood still. A large number of Solar Drakes circled the burning wreckage of the spaceships along with the buildings. The fourth ship, the one that hadn't been broadcasting an identifying signal, was gone. "What happened?"

"His ship took off right after he got into it," Del explained. "I didn't even think to scan it for armaments. But he blasted the other ships before he took off. Somehow, I don't think the school is going to be very happy with us."

The doctor turned to them. "You've managed to get yourselves into a very complex situation here. I don't think many people are going to be happy with you." He sighed. "But Skylar and Filzbalm did manage to save me and the remains of my staff. Let's go see if we can get a distress call out in hopes that someone helpful will show up. Maybe the emergency beacon wasn't damaged."

"Hey, I've got Skylar's Galactic Com unit." Del dug into his pocket and pulled out the device. "I bet we can reach someone on it."

Skylar smiled at his friend—at least they weren't stuck. "Okay, but who do we call? The school? We took Stars' End Beta. They might want to just let us rot out here while they use one of the other school ships to get the kids from the Galaxeria." He looked at Doctor Wellengrad. "Do you have any idea who to call?"

"We could call our home office. They're at the Central Galactic University Campus. It might take them a couple of days to get here." The brown Solar Drake landed on his shoulder.

"Call Uncle Phil," Solaria suggested. "He's got his own ship. He can get here fairly quickly no matter where he is. And he's got some pull at the school, so maybe he can smooth things over. He's a level-ten feeler—if nothing else, he can smooth things over with everyone and make them feel that it would be a bad idea to do too much to us."

In the end, they called Phil and Wellengrad's home office. Both promised to get there as quickly as possible. By then, the Volarian had returned with the two raiders they'd managed to capture. Doctor Palu and Doctor Wells, the Volarian, and the other human, Pam, an intern, secured the Boarisk prisoners, then enlisted Solaria in helping them gather their dead. The Boarisks had killed five of the other researchers when they arrived. Next to each dead researcher was the lifeless body of a Solar Drake.

"Skylar, can I talk to you for a few minutes?" Doctor Wellengrad asked as the others headed back into the jungle. The twilight was already beginning to brighten back to full daylight without going to darkness.

Skylar nodded. He hoped Doctor Wellengrad wasn't about to kill him, then kill his friends. They were on a restricted planet, and in Galactic Explorers, people were always being killed for discovering restricted areas. Although the researcher didn't seem like the type of person to go around killing kids, something in his gut told him the complexity of the Solar Drake's secrets were worth killing over.

"You're in a rather unique situation, Mr. Mars," Doctor Wellengrad began as he put his hands behind his back and took on a thoughtful expression. "You've bonded with a Solar Drake."

"Is that what happened?" He reached up and stroked Filzbalm's head. "Is that why I could sometimes hear him thinking at me even with the dampening bracelet on?"

Doctor Wellengrad's brown eyes grew large. "You had a dampening bracelet on? Why did you have a dampening bracelet on?" He stopped pacing and stared at Skylar.

With a deep breath to steady himself, Skylar began explaining what had happened to him, about how his mother had been killed, how he ended up at Stars' End Academy with a distrust and fear of psychics that he had to overcome before he could properly wield his powers. How he'd occasionally dreamt of inhuman screams, which after learning he could hear Filzbalm, he suspected the screams were that of a Solar Drake mother. He told the researcher how Solaria had rescued the egg, but had been unable to keep it in her room, and how they'd decided to try and bring the fledgling back to his home world.

Doctor Wellengrad was silent for a minute or so after Skylar completed his tale. He stroked the back of the brown drake that lay on his muscular forearm with its tail wrapped around his waist. "That's quite the tale. At least your hearts, those of all three of you, were in the right place. It's true that Solar Drakes don't do well in other environments, but it's not for the reasons that most people think. It's also true that they are attracted to strong readers. They seek to bond with us. When they bond to a reader, part of what we are transfers to them. Even without the bonding, they're still extremely intelligent, but when they join with a reader, that intelligence is multiplied. They understand things we never will.

"But the bonding is not one-sided. They help open up a psychic's talents, sometimes more than doubling a person's mental strength. Are you stronger after the bonding or the same strength you were before you bonded?" Before Skylar could answer, the researcher gestured the question aside. "Never mind—you had a fear of psychics, so you wouldn't know." He sighed. "But now we have to decide what to do with you. You see, one of the reasons this planet is off-limits is to prevent people from bonding with the drakes. Everyone who bonds with a drake has to stay on the Ring."

The words hit Skylar like a slap in the face. He stared at Doctor Wellengrad as his guts balled up, and he felt nauseous. "But I'm just getting used to Stars' End. I'm making friends. I don't know where my life is going, but I don't want to spend it isolated here on this little planet with its strange twilight and humid jungle. I want to explore the galaxy, and maybe the universe. This isn't fair."

Doctor Wellengrad shook his head. "I'm sorry. I don't make the rules. I can never leave the planet either, but my bond with Selvileigh makes it worth it. He completes me in a way that nothing else could."

"No, I can't just stay here. I just flew my first space ship. It was one of the most awesome things I've ever done. If I stay here, I'll never get the chance to do that again." He turned to walk away from Doctor Wellengrad. A strong wave of soothing emotions washed over him.

Skylar spun around and glared at the man. "No!" He thrust the calming energies back in Doctor Wellengrad's face. "You will *not* manipulate me into seeing things your way. Not again. I'm tired of being yanked around by adults who think they know what's best for me." He took off running as fast as he could across the clearing and into the dense jungle beyond. Filzbalm clung to his shoulder and remained oddly silent.

25
Mother Of Drakes

SKYLAR DIDN'T stop running until his legs began to burn. He slowed to a walk, then sat down on one of the massive roots that jutted out at the base of a huge tree. He didn't want to stay there. It didn't make sense. How could the universe be so cruel to him?

"But didn't the universe bring us together?" Filzbalm pushed his head against Skylar's cheek.

Skylar reached up and stroked the drake's head. "Yes, it did, and now that I know it's you who's trying to talk to me and that you're able to help me control my abilities, I appreciate it, but I don't want to be planet bound. I've been in the stars and I want to stay there."

Filzbalm nodded slightly or he might've just been pushing his head harder into Skylar's hand. *"I like it in the stars, too. They make an endless sky, even if we do need the ships to fly across it."*

"And that, my child, is why we fight so hard to keep our children here." A deep female voice filled Skylar's head. He looked up into the branches of the tree and found a pair of brilliant red eyes looking back.

As he stared up, the eyes grew closer. Every so often, as the source of the voice moved down the tree, it would pass from the thick shadows through a spot of soft light, leaving no doubt in Skylar's mind that she was a Solar Drake, but much larger than Filzbalm or any of the others that he'd seen so far. Skylar sat frozen to the root as she came closer to him. His pulse pounded so loud in his ears he wondered if he would be able to hear the next things she said—if she said anything at all before jumping on him and eating him.

When she reached the lowest branch, she walked along it for a moment before her thick, heavy tail whipped up around her front legs. She lay her massive head down on her tail, but continued to stare down at Skylar. In the shadows, it was impossible to see clearly the color of her hide. It kept changing as the dappled light played over it. She was every color he'd so far seen in Solar Drakes, but none had looked the way she did. She was vivid and vibrant, like she was her own color spectrum. *"Skylar Mars and Filzbalm, you two represent a very complex problem for me, one I foresaw back when the eggs were first stolen. I suppose it was only a matter of time before some entrepreneurial person thought to exploit our species. For nearly a thousand years, the treaty we formed with the Central Galactic Council has held."*

Skylar finally found his voice. "And what was that treaty?" He couldn't say why, but he knew this drake was extremely old and extremely powerful. Knowing that didn't help push back the fear inside him.

"That I would keep my children here on the Ring and we would never leave the Armstrong system. I would've preferred that the council leave us in peace. Particularly after I saw what exposure to your readers did to my kind. There is such a thing as too smart. But the drive to explore is stronger. It was wrong of me, perhaps." She slowly shook her head, and a feeling of sadness rolled off her. *"I'm happy here on the Ring, as your people call our planetoids. I just call them home. But in exchange for keeping us isolated, I agreed to let a small research facility be built here so the council would know if any of my children left the world. They are the council's eyes and ears here.*

"For many years things have been quiet. People respected our isolation. There was only a bare minimum of information released. Even on tours of the research facility, it was never revealed that your kind and mine could bond. We specifically asked that no strong telepaths, beyond the research team, be allowed on the planet. From time to time, one would slip through our screening, like you did. Your friend Del is very smart. An excellent example of his species."

Skylar chuckled nervously. "I'll tell him that." Skylar began to wonder where his conversation with the drake was going. It was nice to know part of where the prohibitions on travel to and from the world came from, but it didn't explain everything, like what was going to happen to him.

"So, you want to know what I will do with you?"

"Yes." Skylar nodded as he struggled to keep the fear out of his voice. "That would be nice to know."

"I would very much like to continue to go out into space, Mother Of Us All." Filzbalm stood tall on Skylar's shoulder and rested his forelegs on the top of Skylar's head. The little drake's courage at speaking so strongly to the much larger drake helped push some of Skylar's fears back, and he relaxed slightly. *"Skylar would be good to travel with. He's a very special young man, at least compared to the others at his school. He also chooses his companions very well."*

"I agree that he does choose very good companions." She tilted her head slightly and peered at Skylar through just one eye. Her gaze sent shivers through him. It felt like she was looking more deeply into him than anyone ever had. All that he'd ever known or experienced was laid bare for her. It took everything he had to stand there and allow her to study him.

When she blinked, the feeling vanished. *"Yes, you are a remarkable young man who has a mark to leave on this galaxy and beyond. And you, young Filzbalm, have much to contribute as well. I don't think it would do my people good for you to remain among them. You've seen too much in your short life. You know more than just our jungle. I think you would stir a wanderlust in others that might well be the undoing I have sought to prevent."*

She sighed. *"When the others from your academy arrive, I shall speak with them, and I advise Doctor Wellengrad of the exception being made to the treaty."* She uncurled her tail and stood. *"Don't make me regret my decision. I also set you a task, one that may not be easy. In your travels, when you meet Filzbalm's brother, send him home. He and his human will not be allowed to return to space. They are too dangerous. Already I can feel the disturbances they create."* Without unfurling her wings, she ascended the tree and vanished from sight into the thick canopy.

Skylar sat there on the root, more questions running through his mind that he wished he'd asked. Somehow, he knew that when he saw her next, he wasn't going to get the opportunity to ask personal questions. Still, he sighed happily. "We get to return to space."

"Yes," Filzbalm agreed. *"It'll be a most exciting life that we shall live."*

"I think exciting will be a good start." Skylar looked up through an opening in the jungle canopy. The second planetoid shone bright and green against a background of stellar dust. A huge river cut through the green. It was one of the most unique sights he'd ever heard of in the galaxy, and he got to see it. If he had any say in it, it was going to be just the start of the amazing and wondrous things he was going to see as he explored the universe. With Filzbalm on his shoulder and his powers under control, there was nothing he couldn't do.

26
Ramifications

SKYLAR SET his plate in the small sink in the back room of the research station as Del came running in. "Solaria's Uncle Phil has entered orbit. He'll be here in a little while."

"That's good." Skylar ran water over the plate. The simple chore made him think of being home with his mother.

He frowned. He'd been too late to prevent another mother from dying as she'd protected her young. Doctor Wellengrad had assured him that the eggs were going to be fine. The father drake had survived, and some of the younger drakes in the forest who didn't have nests at the time were more than willing to help him incubate the eggs. The researchers would help make sure the babies grew up just fine. Since they had all already bonded to other drakes, there wasn't a risk of them bonding to any of the other ones in their care. One drake to one reader, that was the way things worked, and since they didn't bond to feelers or movers, none of the others had anything to worry about. Even Phil would be safe to come to the Ring.

Doctor Wellengrad walked in as Skylar dried his plate. "She's asking that we speak with your Philaneo when he arrives. She says if it's all right with the Central Galactic Council, he and I can negotiate with her to amend the treaty." He leaned against the counter next to Skylar. "I never thought I'd see the day when the treaty would be renegotiated."

"I'm sorry I caused this problem," Skylar said, setting the dish towel on the counter.

"But you saved Filzbalm." Doctor Wellengrad put his hand on Skylar's shoulder. "And you and your friends were doing the right thing by trying to bring him back. I'm not sure even your teachers at Stars' End would've known what to do if you'd taken a Solar Drake to them. You might not have used the right methods to get him back here, but you did try."

"It's all we could do," Skylar replied.

"Got a ship landing," Melody said as she rushed in. "Guess we get to go home."

"You're not a reader," Doctor Wellengrad said. "You wouldn't have had to stay anyway."

"Oh." She looked at Skylar. "They swore us to secrecy about this place. I guess that's better than having my memory wiped."

"Definitely," Del said. "But we're going to keep our mouths shut about all the other drakes here, even with Filzbalm staying with us at school."

Skylar sighed and missed Filzbalm's weight on his shoulder. The little drake was out in the forest, had said something about wanting to speak to the Mother of All for a while before it was time to go. "At least he's getting to go with us. That's the important thing."

"It is," Wellengrad agreed. "Now, you said Philaneo is a Pantherian, like Solaria. To make things easier on them, I've set up a room with some air conditioning so we can all talk and they won't have to wear envirosuits. I left word for Philaneo to land next to that building." He got a faraway look. "Drakes are coming out of the jungle. We'd better head to the room and get ready."

As they entered the hall adjoining the room with air-conditioning, the air filled with the flapping of delicate leather wings as the drakes swarmed the building, led by Filzbalm.

Skylar held out his arm and Filzbalm landed there before running up to his shoulder.

"She wants me to report back every week on what I have learned. We don't have to come here, simply sending a report to Doctor Wellengrad will be fine. She trusts him more than any human who has ever led the researchers before him. I think she just wants to make sure we're staying out of trouble."

"Probably." Skylar laughed as the familiar form of Phil entered the building. He was droopy and moving slowly in the heat, but wasn't wearing an envirosuit. Behind him stood the sleek, bald form of Professor Aduncus. The professor didn't feel happy. Skylar swallowed hard.

"You must be Philaneo." Doctor Wellengrad stepped up to Phil and offered him his hand.

"Doctor Wellengrad." Phil returned the handshake, then frowned at Skylar. "Allow me to introduce Professor Aduncus from Stars' End Academy. He was with me when I received the call to come here."

Doctor Wellengrad's eyes widened. "Professor Aduncus, I've heard of you. You're one of the most powerful readers around."

Professor Aduncus held up his arm, displaying a dampening bracelet identical to the one Skylar had been wearing for weeks and that was still in Del's pocket. "And I have blinded myself to retrieve my students." He glared hardest at Del. "Although I may leave my grandson here in your care."

Del rolled his eyes. "Oh, come on, Grandfather. We were just trying to do the right thing."

"And sometimes that's not enough," Professor Aduncus said solemnly. "The universe has rules for a reason. We will be discussing many of those before we leave the planet, and on the way back to school."

Skylar didn't like the sound of that but kept his mouth and mind closed.

"Please, gentlemen, let's go into the room we've set up to accommodate Philaneo and Solaria while we discuss the matters at hand." Doctor Wellengrad swept his arm toward the front room off the hall. "We are sorry for the tight accommodations, but we do our best to limit disrupting the environment here, so we try to not cool rooms more than we need to. The smaller the room, the less we disrupt."

"That's fine," Phil said as they entered the room. "I just want to get out of this heat. Due to my travels with Intergal, I can tolerate it more than most of my people, but this is pressing even on me."

"Uncle Phil!" Solaria hollered and threw herself at him. She was out of her envirosuit and looked a lot better than she had earlier.

Happiness rolled off both of them as they hugged. Skylar felt a little jealous. Solaria had a loving family while he still missed his mother very much, and often wondered if the pain of her loss would ever lessen.

Filzbalm landed on his shoulder. *"You've got me. I might not be a mother, but I'll never leave you. We are together now, forever."*

"I know." Skylar reached up and stroked the drake's head. He recalled the sights of the dead researchers, each with a lifeless drake at their side. The researchers had been shot, but the drakes had no injuries that he'd been able to see in his quick look. It was as if they'd just died when their bondmates had perished. He hadn't taken the time to confirm that with Doctor Wellengrad. He didn't like the idea that if something happened to him, Filzbalm would share his fate, but it was too late to turn back. They'd bonded and that was that.

"All right." Phil released Solaria and turned to the rest of them. "Would someone please explain exactly what is going on here? Our communication was brief when you lot called for help."

"Well…" Skylar felt it was his place to start. He began with Solaria taking the egg from Pathal and didn't stop talking until he got to the point where they'd gotten a hold of Phil and he'd agreed to come rescue them.

"I thought there was something you three have been hiding," Professor Aduncus said. "I have to say that I'm not overly surprised. I've been feeling a presence in school that I couldn't identify. I've consulted with Ms. Grissom and the other teachers who are high enough levels to feel more than just the basic emotions and thoughts you students put out. We knew there was something amiss, but we couldn't put our fingers on what it was. We even consulted a seer, and she couldn't help."

Doctor Wellengrad laughed hard enough that he doubled over in his chair. Everyone stopped and stared at him.

He coughed a couple of times to stop the laughter. "I'm sorry. The idea of using a seer to find out anything about Solar Drakes is ludicrous, but you couldn't have known what you were dealing with at the time. Solar Drakes confuse seers. We aren't sure exactly what it is about them, but the couple of times we've had highly skilled seers stop by for research, it's like they couldn't even see a drake when they're in the same room with one."

Professor Aduncus rubbed his chin. "That's most interesting. I don't suppose there's any chance you'd share your research with me? I promise you I can keep it to myself. Since it appears Filzbalm is going to be attending school with young Mr. Mars, it might be in all of our interests to know as much as we can about him."

"And that brings us to one of the reasons we're all in this room," Doctor Wellengrad said as he walked over to one of the simple wooden chairs and settled there. "The

Mother of All Drakes has asked that we renegotiate the treaty that prevents the people who bond with Solar Drakes from leaving the Armstrong system. She is ready to allow Filzbalm and Skylar to return to Stars' End Academy, and after that, lead the life they choose to lead, but there will be conditions."

Phil and Professor Aduncus frowned at the same time.

"What kind of conditions?" Phil asked first.

Doctor Wellengrad huffed. "Are you all right with my acting as her emissary in this, and is our Galactic Council accepting of your acting on their behalf?"

Professor Aduncus produced a small holographic projector. "We were in contact with the Council on our way here." He tapped the projector and the form of a tall human female appeared.

Skylar's breath caught. It was the current president of the Council. He recognized Carolyn Cranby from history class. She'd been serving as president for twenty years, and had made a lot of reforms to the council during that time. Although she had a lot of enemies, she was still in charge.

"Hello," the hologram began in a crisp, clear voice. "In terms of the Armstrong Treaty, something I was very surprised to learn about, I am prepared to allow Philaneo Clawson to act as an emissary of the Central Galactic Council, to renegotiate a minor clause in the treaty. It is my understanding that we are not renegotiating the entire treaty, just one clause. Should we require more than that, I may need to contact the entire council." The hologram cut off.

Doctor Wellengrad nodded. "I don't think we need to totally renegotiate the entire treaty."

"Very well." Phil settled across the narrow table from Doctor Wellengrad.

Skylar plopped into a chair next to Del, with Solaria and Melody nearby. It was a shame that he and Filzbalm were causing so much trouble, but if it would help him keep the life he was growing used to and keep Filzbalm, he was all for it. He just hoped things wouldn't take forever. It had been a long day, and after the good meal he'd eaten with the researchers, he was ready for a bit of sleep.

BY THE time Phil, Professor Aduncus, and Doctor Wellengrad had worked out the details of the amended clause, everyone was ready to fall asleep. It was all Skylar could do to stay awake as Phil piloted his ship through the Armstrong system, heading for the restricted stargate.

"Now that we have the galactic law part of this settled," Professor Aduncus said, drawing Skylar's bleary gaze from the stars.

Del yawned. "Oh, come on Grandfather, can't this wait? It's been a tumultuous day."

Professor Aduncus removed his dampening bracelet, which was a little different from Skylar's—it could be taken off with one hand. He sighed and rubbed his temples. "Yes, Del, it has been a long day, and as soon as I convey your sentence you can get some rest. Trust me, you're going to need all the relaxation you can get."

"I don't think he's as angry as he's acting," Filzbalm said softly. *"His thoughts are too organized for anger."*

"And if he catches you reading his mind he's going to get really upset," Skylar replied.

"Look, this was all my idea," Solaria said, stepping between him and them. "Skylar and Del were just going along with me to get the Solar Drake, Filzbalm, home. Melody got scooped up in the whole mess when we stole the ship."

"I know all this," Professor Aduncus said. "And the fact that you're stepping up and being honest will go down in the school records, Miss Unica. We are still trying to figure out who's going to pay for the Stars' End Beta."

"Hey." Skylar straightened, his sleepiness suddenly forgotten. "We didn't blow up the ship. That Boarisk captain did."

Professor Aduncus nodded slowly. "But the ship wouldn't have been in danger if the three of you hadn't stolen it in the first place and taken it to Armstrong's Ring."

Skylar didn't see a way he could argue that point. He slumped and stayed quiet.

"But at this point, a bill has been sent to the Boarisk Confederation. We don't expect them to pay it, since they are a non-psi race and have never contributed to the funding of Stars' End Academy." He spread his hands in a hopeless gesture. "Regardless, we will try, and will file a grievance when they refuse to pay. The odds are our insurance will cover the cost of replacing the ship. But we will have to make an example of the four of you after this escapade."

"Wait, Melody shouldn't be part of this. She was just on the ship when we took it," Skylar and Solaria objected at the same time. If it had been any other corp-brat but Melody, Skylar would've kept his mouth shut, but she'd proven to be willing to help out. Maybe he'd been judging the corp-brats too harshly. He didn't think she deserved trouble for being in the wrong place at the wrong time.

"But remember, this is for an example," Professor Aduncus continued. "We can't have the whole school thinking they can just steal a ship and get away with it. The fact is, Ms. Porsche has a dermal communicator, as do you all. She could've reported your activities the second she discovered what you were doing. She did not. Therefore, she is guilty by association."

Skylar looked over his shoulder to where Melody slumped in her chair. She'd been strangely quiet since leaving Armstrong's Ring. In all the excitement, he hadn't stopped to think that she could've turned them all in at any time. If it had been Pathal or most of the others, they would've done it in a heartbeat, just to cause trouble.

"So, all of your parents have been notified of your little jaunt across space. We have chosen, due to the terms of the Treaty of Armstrong to not go into details about your adventure. For the next three months, until third quarter break, you are all confined to the station. No field trips, no shopping trips. The only reason you'll be allowed off station is for family emergencies, and then only if your parents come and pick you up."

Skylar suppressed a sigh. He didn't have any family, not anymore. But three months on the station wasn't going to be horrible. He could get through it.

"In addition, you are all going to be assigned farm detail after classes every day. You'll go to the farm and garden area and do whatever tasks Mrs. Clementine, our farm curator, and her staff see fit. If your grades fall, there will be additional study-related penalties." He turned his steely gaze to Skylar. "And Mr. Mars, you will also do one hour of practice with me every day after you finish your farm detail. We're going to have to get your powers under control. Even if young Filzbalm can act as your dampening bracelet, I won't have you losing control again. It sounds like you had a very close call with the Boarisk." Then he looked at Solaria. "And there will be no extracurricular activities such as Z-GBall until your sentence is over. None of you is to even set foot in the center of the station. Do I make myself clear?"

"Yes, Professor Aduncus," they all said in unison. Even Filzbalm added his mental consent.

Professor Aduncus nodded solemnly, then walked up to the flight deck, leaving them alone.

Skylar sank into one of the clothes-covered chairs. He was a little surprised Phil hadn't taken the time to clean up the ship before coming to rescue them, particularly since he had Professor Aduncus along.

Del sighed and settled in the chair next to him. "That could've gone worse."

"Yeah, it could've." Solaria sat on the floor, in one of the clean spots in the rear cabin. "We could've all been expelled."

"That would've been my luck," Melody said from her seat. "I'm not sure what my mom would've done then."

"But we weren't expelled," Skylar said. The fatigue he'd been feeling came roaring back, and he yawned. "We're going to stay in school, and three months isn't too long to work out at the farm. The place kinda reminds me of Hummassa. If we work at it, we can make it fun." He wasn't sure where he would've gone if they'd thrown him out, but it didn't matter. He was going to stay in school. He was getting to keep Filzbalm. Everything was going to be great.

Outside the window, the lights from the stargate flared. Skylar didn't have a great view, but it didn't really matter. There would be other chances to go through stargates. He was going to visit every world he could. He and Filzbalm were going to explore the universe and report back to The Mother of All Drakes about their adventures.

Glancing at Del and Solaria, he hoped they'd want to come along too. They all had their whole lives ahead of them, and he wanted to make sure his was a grand adventure.

Who is Drew Seren?

Drew Seren was raised on a diet of science fiction, both in print and on the screen. He spent many nights watching Star Trek and Space 1999 with his father. Comic books were a main staple of his reading, and then when he was in high school he started reading *Dragon Riders of Pern* and quickly began devouring any science fiction he could, luckily his father had an extensive library at the time. He started writing soon after that, letting writing help him make it through class. During college and his corporate life, Drew spent a lot of time writing to help him endure the mundane things that gnawed at him. Through his twenties and thirties, comic books and science fiction helped him survive. To this day, he's still reading as much or more than he's writing. He's also an avid gamer, playing first *Dungeons and Dragons*, and currently lots of *World of Warcraft*. He's recently turned his attention to writing full time and exploring the vast galaxy through new and interesting eyes.

Stay in touch with Drew through his website
www.drewseren.com

and Facebook pages
fb.me/drewseren

Feel free to drop Drew an email
drew@drewseren.com